# Fern's Hollow by Hesba Stretton

Hesba Stretton was the pen name of Sarah Smith who was born on July 27th 1832 in Wellington, Shropshire, the younger daughter of bookseller, Benjamin Smith and his wife, Anne Bakewell Smith, a devout Methodist. Although she and her elder sister attended the Old Hall school in town, they were largely self-educated.

Smith became one of the most popular Evangelical writers of the 19th century. She used her "Christian principles as a protest against specific social evils in her children's books." Her moral tales and semi-religious stories, mainly directed towards the young, were printed in huge numbers.

After her sister submitted, without her knowledge, a story on her behalf ('The Lucky Leg', was a bizarre tale of a widower who proposes to women with wooden legs) Smith became a regular contributor to Household Words and All the Year Round, two popular periodicals begun by Charles Dickens. Dickens would collaborate with many writers to produce his part-work stories. Smith writing under the pseudonym Hesba Stretton (created from the initials of herself and four surviving siblings: **H**annah, **E**lizabeth, **S**arah, **B**enjamin, **A**nna and the name of a Shropshire village; All Stretton) contributed a well-regarded short story, 'The Ghost in the Cloak-Room', as part of 'The Haunted House'. She would go on to write over 40 novels.

Her break out book was 'Jessica's First Prayer', published in the Sunday at Home journal in 1866 and the following year as a book. By the end of the century it had sold over one and a half million copies. To put that into context; ten times the sales of 'Alice in Wonderland'. The book gave rise to a strand of books about homeless children in Victorian society combining elements of the sensational novel and the religious tract bringing the image of the poor, under-privileged, child into the Victorian social conscious.

A sequel, 'Jessica's Mother', was published in Sunday at Home in 1866 and eventually as a book, some decades later, in 1904. It was translated into fifteen European and Asiatic languages as well as Braille, depicted on coloured slides for magic lantern segments of Bands of Hope programmes, and placed in all Russian schools by order of Tsar Alexander II.

Smith became the chief writer for the Religious Tract Society. Her experience of working with slum children in Manchester in the 1860s gave her books great atmosphere and, of course, a sense of authenticity.

In 1884, Smith was one of the co-founders, together with Lord Shaftesbury and others, of the London Society for the Prevention of Cruelty to Children, which then combined, five years later, with societies in other cities to form the National Society for the Prevention of Cruelty to Children. Smith resigned a decade later in protest at financial mismanagement.

In retirement in Richmond, Surrey, the Smith sisters ran a branch of the Popular Book Club for working-class readers.

Sarah Smith died on October 8th, 1911 at home at Ivycroft on Ham Common. She had survived her sister by eight months.

# Index of Contents

CHAPTER I

THE HUT IN THE HOLLOW

Just upon the border of Wales, but within one of the English counties, there is a cluster of hills, rising one above the other in gradual slopes, until the summits form a long, broad tableland, many miles across. This tableland is not so flat that all of it can be seen at once, but here and there are little dells, shaped like deep basins, which the country folk call hollows; and every now and then there is a rock or hillock covered with yellow gorse bushes, from the top of which can be seen the wide, outspread plains, where hundreds of sheep and ponies are feeding, which belong to the farmers and cottagers dwelling in the valley below. Besides the chief valley, which divides the mountains into two groups, and which is broad enough for a village to be built in, there are long, narrow glens, stretching up into the very heart of the tableland, and draining away the waters which gather there by the melting of snow in the winter and the rain of thunderstorms in summer. Down every glen flows a noisy mountain stream, dashing along its rocky course with so many tiny waterfalls and impatient splashes, that the gurgling and bubbling of brooks come up even into the quietness of the tableland and mingle with the singing of the birds and the humming of the bees among the heather. There are not many paths across the hills, except the narrow sheep-walks worn by the tiny feet of the sheep as they follow one another in long, single lines, winding in and out through the clumps of gorse; and few people care to explore the solitary plains, except the shepherds who have the charge of the flocks, and tribes of village children who go up every summer to gather the fruit of the wild and hardy bilberry wires.

The whole of this broad tableland, as well as the hills, are common pasture for the inhabitants of the valleys, who have an equal right to keep sheep and ponies on the uplands with the lord of the manor. But the property of the soil belongs to the latter, and he only has the power of enclosing the waste so as to make fields and plant woods upon it, provided always that he leaves a sufficient portion for the use of the villagers. In times gone by, however, when the lord of the manor and his agent were not very watchful, it was the practice of poor persons, who did not care how uncomfortably they lived, to seek out some distant hollow, or the farthest and most hidden side of a hillock, and there build themselves such a low, small hut, as should escape the notice of any passer-by, should they chance to go that way. Little by little, making low fences which looked like the surrounding gorse bushes, they enclosed small portions of the waste land, or, as it is called, encroached upon the common; and if they were able to keep their encroachment without having their hedges broken down, or if the lord of the manor neglected to demand rent for it for the space of twenty years, their fields and gardens became securely and legally their own. Because of this right, therefore, are to be found here and there little farms of three or four fields a-piece, looking like islands, with the wide, open common around them; and some miles away over the breezy uplands there is even a little hamlet of these poor cottages, all belonging to the people who dwell in them.

Many years ago, even many years before my story begins, a poor woman—who was far worse off than a widow, for her husband had just been sentenced to transportation for twenty-one years—strayed down to these mountains upon her sorrowful way home to her native place. She had her only child with her, a boy five years of age; and from some reason or other, perhaps because she could not bear to go home in shame and disgrace, she sought out a very lonely hiding-place among the hills, and with her own hands reared rough walls of turf and stones, until she had formed such a rude hut as would just give shelter to her and her boy. There they lived, uncared for and solitary, until the husband came back, after suffering his twenty-one years' punishment, and entered into a little spot of land entirely his own. Then, with the assistance of his son, a strong, full-grown young man, he rebuilt the cottage, though upon a scale not much larger or much more commodious than his wife's old hut.

Like other groups of mountains, the highest and largest are those near the centre, and from them the land descends in lower and lower levels, with smaller hills and smoother valleys, until at length it sinks into the plain. Then they are almost like children's hills and valleys; the slopes are not too steep for very little feet to climb, and the rippling brooks are not in so much hurry to rush on to the distant river, but that boys and girls at play can stop them for a little time with slight banks of mud and stones. In just such a smooth, sloping dell, down in a soft green basin, called Fern's Hollow, was the hiding-place where the convict's sad wife had found an unmolested shelter.

This dwelling, the second one raised by the returned convict and his son, is built just below the brow of the hill, so that the back of the hut is formed of the hill itself, and only the sides and front are real walls. These walls are made of rubble, or loose, unhewn stones, piled together with a kind of mortar, which is little more than clay baked hard in the heat of the sun. The chimney is a bit of old stove-pipe, scarcely rising above the top of the hill behind; and, but for the smoke, we could look down the pipe, as through the tube of a telescope, upon the family sitting round the hearth within. The thatch, overgrown with moss, appears as a continuation of the slope of the hill itself, and might almost deceive the simple sheep grazing around it. Instead of a window there is only a square hole, covered by a shutter when the light is not urgently needed; and the door is so much too small for its sill and lintels as to leave large chinks, through which adventurous bees and beetles may find their way within. You may see at a glance that there is but one room, and that there can be no up-stairs to the hut, except that upper storey of the broad, open common behind it, where the birds sleep softly in their cosy nests. Before the house is a garden; and beyond that a small field sown with silver oats, which are dancing and glistening in the breeze and sunshine; while before the garden wicket, but not enclosed from the common, is a warm, sunny valley, in the very middle of which a slender thread of a brook widens into a lovely little basin of a pool, clear and cold, the very place for the hill ponies to come and drink.

Looking steadily up this pleasant valley from the threshold of the cottage, we can just see a fine, light film of white smoke against the blue sky. Two miles away, right down off the mountains, there is a small coal-field and a quarry of limestone. In a distant part of the country there are large tracts of land where coal and iron pits are sunk on every side, and their desolate and barren pit-banks extend for miles round, while a heavy cloud of smoke hangs always in the air. But here, just at the foot of these mountains, there is one little seam of coal, as if placed for the express use of these people, living so far away from the larger coal-fields. The Botfield lime and coal works cover only a few acres of the surface; but underground there are long passages bored beneath the pleasant pastures and the yellow cornfields. From the mountains, Botfield looks rather like a great blot upon the fair landscape, with its blackened engine-house and banks of coal-dust, its long range of limekilns, sultry and quivering in the summer sunshine, and its heavy, groaning water-wheel, which pumps up the water from the pits below. But the colliers do not think it so, nor their wives in the scattered village beyond; they do not consider the lime and coal works a blot, for their living depends upon them, and they may rightly say, 'As for the earth, out of it cometh bread: and under it is turned up as it were fire.'

Even Stephen Fern, who would a thousand times rather work out on the free hillside than in the dark passages underground, does not think it a pity that the Botfield pit has been discovered at the foot of the mountains. It is nearly seven o'clock in the evening, and he is coming over the brow of the green dell, with his long shadow stretching down it. A very long shadow it is for so small a figure to cast, for if we wait a minute or two till Stephen draws nearer, we shall see that he is no strong, large man, but a slight, thin, stooping boy, bending rather wearily under a sack of coals, which he is carrying on his shoulders, and pausing now and then to wipe his heated forehead with the sleeve of his collier's flannel jacket. When he lifts up the latch of his home we will enter with him, and see the inside of the hut at Fern's Hollow.


## CHAPTER II

### THE DYING FATHER

Stephen stepped over the threshold into a low, dark room, which was filled with smoke, from a sudden gust of the wind as it swept over the roof of the hut. On one side of the grate, which was made of some half-hoops of iron fastened into the rock, there was a very aged man, childish and blind with years, who was crouching towards the fire, and talking and chuckling to himself. A girl, about a year older than Stephen, sat in a rocking-chair, and swung to and fro as she knitted away fast and diligently at a thick grey stocking. In the corner nearest to the fireplace there stood a pallet-bed, hardly raised above the earthen floor, to which Stephen hastened immediately, with an anxious look at the thin, white face of his father lying upon the pillow. Beside the sick man there lay a little child fast asleep, with her hand clasping one of her father's fingers; and though James Fern was shaking and trembling with a violent fit of coughing from the sudden gust of smoke, he took care not to loose the hold of those tiny fingers.

'Poor little Nan!' he whispered to Stephen, as soon as he could speak. 'I've been thinking all day of her and thee, lad, till I'm nigh heart-broken.'

'Do you feel worse, father?' asked Stephen anxiously.

'I'm drawing nearer the end,' answered James Fern,—'nearer the end every hour; and I don't know for certain what the end will be. I'm repenting; but I can't undo the mischief I've done; I must leave that behind me. If I'd been anything like a decent father, I should have left you comfortable, instead of poor beggars. And what is to become of my poor lass here? See how fast she clips my hand, as if she was afeared I was going to leave her! Oh, Stephen, my lad, what will you all do?'

'Father,' said Stephen, in a quiet and firm voice, 'I'm getting six shillings a week wages, and we can live on very little. We haven't got any rent to pay, and only ourselves and grandfather to keep, and Martha is as good as a woman grown. We'll manage, father, and take care of little Nan.'

'Stephen and I are not bad, father,' added Martha, speaking up proudly; 'I am not like Black Bess of Botfield. Mother always told me I was to do my duty; and I always do it. I can wash, and sew, and iron, and bake, and knit. Why, often and often we've had no more than Stephen's earnings, when you've been to the Red Lion on reckoning nights.'

'Hush, hush, Martha!' whispered Stephen.

'No, it's true,' groaned the dying father; 'God Almighty, have mercy on me! Stephen, hearken to me, and thee too, Martha, while I tell you about this place, and what you are to do when I'm gone.'

He paused for a minute or two, looking earnestly at the crouching old man in the chimney-corner.

'Grandfather's quite simple,' he said, 'and he's dark, too, and doesn't know what any one is saying. But I know thee'lt be good to him, Stephen. Hearken, children: your poor old grandfather was once in jail, and was sent across the seas, for a thief.'

'Father!' cried Stephen, in a tone of deep distress; and he turned quickly to the old man, remembering how often he had sat upon his knees by the winter fire, and how many summer days he had rambled with him over the uplands after the sheep. His grandfather had been far kinder to him than his own father; and his heart swelled with anger as he went and laid his arm round the bending neck of the old man, who looked up in his face and laughed heartily.

'Come back, Stephen; it's true,' gasped James Fern. 'Poor mother and me came here, where nobody knew us, while he was away for more than twenty years; and she built a hut for-us to live in till he came back. I was a little lad then, but as soon as I was big enough she made me learn to read and write, that I might send letters to him beyond the seas and none of the neighbours know. She'd often make me read to her about a poor fellow who had left home and gone to a far country, and when he came home again, how his father saw him a long way off. Well, she was just like that when she'd heard that he was landed in England; she did nought but sit over the bent of the hill yonder, peering along the road to Botfield; and one evening at sundown she saw something, little more than a speck upon the turf, and she'd a feeling come over her that it was he, and she fainted for real joy. After all, we weren't much happier when we were settled down like. Grandfather had learned to tend sheep out yonder, and I worked at Botfield; but we never laid by money to build a brick house, as poor mother always wanted us. She died a month or so afore I was married to your mother.'

James Fern was silent again for some minutes, leaning back upon his pillow, with his eyes closed, and his thoughts gone back to the old times.

'If I'd only been like mother, you'd have been a hill-farmer now, Steve,' he continued, in a tone of regret; 'she plotted out in her own mind to take in the green before us, for rearing young lambs, and ducks, and goslings. But I was like that poor lad that wasted all his substance in riotous living; and I've let thee and thy sister grow up without even the learning I could have given thee; and learning is light carriage. But, lad, remember this house is thy own, and never part with it; never give it up, for it is thy right. Maybe they'll want to turn thee out, because thee art a boy; but I've lived in it nigh upon forty years, and I've written it all down upon this piece of paper, and that the place is thine, Stephen.'

'I'll never give it up, father,' said Stephen, in his steady voice.

'Stephen,' continued his father, 'the master has set his heart upon it to make it a hill-farm; and thou'lt have hard work to hold thy own against him. Thou must frame thy words well when he speaks to thee about it, for he's a cunning man. And there's another paper, which the parson at Danesford has in his keeping, to certify that mother built this house and dwelt in it all the days of her life, more than thirty years; if there's any mischief worked against thee, go to him for it. And now, Stephen, wash thyself, and get thy supper, and then let's hear thee read thy chapter.'

Stephen carried his basin of potatoes to the door-sill and sat there, with his back turned to the dismal hut and his dying father, and his face looking out upon the green hills. He had always been a grave and thoughtful boy; and he had much to think of now. The deep sense of new duties and obligations that had come upon him with his father's words, made him feel that his boyhood had passed away. He looked round upon the garden, and the field, and the hut, with the keen eye of an owner; and he wondered at the neglected state into which they had fallen since his father's illness. There could be no more play-time for him; no bird's-nesting among the gorse-bushes; no rabbit-bunting with Snip, the little white terrier that was sharing his supper. If little Nan and his grandfather were to be provided for, he must be a man, with a man's thoughtfulness, doing man's work. There seemed enough work for him to do in the field and garden alone, without his twelve hours' toil in the coal-pit; but his weekly wages would now be more necessary than ever. He must get up early, and go to bed late, and labour without a moment's rest, doing his utmost from one day to another, with no one to help him, or stand for a little while in his place. For a few minutes his brave spirit sank within him, and all the landscape swam before his eyes; while Snip took advantage of his master's inattention to put his nose into the basin, and help himself to the largest share of the potatoes.

'I mean to be like grandmother,' said Martha's clear, sharp voice, close beside him, and he saw his sister looking eagerly round her. 'I shall fence the green in, and have lambs and sheep to turn out on the hillside, and I'll rear young goslings and ducks for market; and we'll have a brick house, with two rooms in it, as well as a shed for the coal. And nobody shall put upon us, or touch our rights, Stephen, or they shall have the length of my tongue.'

'Martha,' said Stephen earnestly, 'do you see how a shower is raining down on the master's fields at Botfield; and they've been scorched up for want of water?'

'Yes, surely,' answered Martha; 'and what of that?'

'I'm thinking,' continued Stephen, rather shyly, 'of that verse in my chapter: "He maketh the sun to rise on the evil and the good, and sendeth rain on the just and the unjust." What sort of a man is the master, Martha?'

'He's a bad, unjust, niggardly old miser,' replied Martha.

'And if God sends him rain, and takes care of him,' Stephen said, 'how much more care will He take of us, if we are good, and try to do His commandments!'

'I should think,' said Martha, but in a softer tone, 'I should really think He would give us the green, and the lambs, and the new house, and everything; for both of us are good, Stephen.'

'I don't know,' replied Stephen; 'if I could read all the Bible, perhaps it would tell us. But now I must go in and read my chapter to father.'

Martha went back to her rocking-chair and knitting, while Stephen reached down from a shelf an old Bible, covered with green baize, and, having carefully looked that his hard hands were quite clean, he opened it with the greatest reverence. James Fern had only begun to teach the boy to read a few months before, when he felt the first fatal symptoms of his illness; and Stephen, with his few opportunities for learning, had only mastered one chapter, the fifth chapter of St. Matthew's Gospel, which his father had chosen for him to begin with. The sick man lay still with closed eyes, but listening attentively to every word, and correcting his son whenever he made any mistake. When it was finished, James Fern read a few verses aloud himself, with low voice and frequent pauses to regain his strength; and very soon afterwards the whole family were in a deep sleep, except himself.

## CHAPTER III

### STEPHEN'S FIRST VICTORY

James Fern did not live many more days, and he was buried the Sunday following his death. All the colliers and pitmen from Botfield walked with the funeral of their old comrade and made a great burial of it. The parish church was two miles on the other side of Botfield, and four miles from Fern's Hollow; so James Fern and his family had never, as he called it, 'troubled' the church with their attendance. All the household, even to little Nan, went with their father's corpse, to bury it in the strange and distant churchyard. Stephen felt as if he was in some long and painful dream, as he sat in the cart, with his feet resting upon his father's coffin, with his grandfather on a chair at the head, nodding and laughing at every jolt on the rough road, and Martha holding a handkerchief up to her face, and carrying a large umbrella over herself and little Nan, to keep the dust off their new black bonnets. The boy, grave as he was, could hardly think; he felt in too great a maze for that. The church, too, which he had never entered before, seemed grand and cold and immense, with its lofty arches, and a roof so high that it made him giddy to look up to it. Now and then he heard a few sentences of the burial service sounding out grandly in the clergyman's strange, deep voice; but they were not words he was familiar with, and he could not understand their meaning. At the open grave only, the clergyman said 'Our Father,' which his father had taught him during his illness; and while his tears rolled down his cheeks for the first time that day, Stephen repeated over and over again to himself, 'Our Father! our Father!'

Stephen would have liked to stay in the church for the evening service, for which the bells were already ringing; but this did not at all suit the tastes of his father's old comrades. They made haste to crowd into a public-house, where they sat and drank, and forced Stephen to drink too, in order to 'drown his grief.' It was still a painful dream to him; and more and more, as the long hours passed on, he wondered how he came there, and what all the people about him were doing. It was quite dark before they started homewards, and the poor old grandfather was no longer able to sit up in his chair, but lay helplessly at the bottom of the cart. Even Martha was fast asleep, and leaned her head upon Stephen's shoulder, without any regard for her new black bonnet. The cart was now crowded with as many of the people as could get into it, who sang and shouted along the quiet Sunday road; and, as they insisted upon stopping at every public-house they came to, it was very late before they reached the lane leading up to Fern's Hollow. The grandfather was half dragged and half carried along by two of the men, followed by Stephen bearing sleepy little Nan in his arms, and by Martha, who had wakened up in a temper between crying and scolding. The long, strange, painful dream of father's funeral was not over yet, and Stephen was still trying to think in a stupid, drowsy fashion, when he fell heavily asleep on the bed beside his grandfather.

He awoke by habit very early in the morning, and aroused himself with a great effort against dropping asleep again. He could realize and understand his position better now. Father was dead; and there was no one to earn bread for them all but himself. At this thought he sprang up instantly, though his head was aching in a manner he had never felt before. With some difficulty he awoke Martha to get his breakfast and put up his dinner in a basket which he carried with him to the pit. She also complained bitterly of her head aching, and moved about with a listlessness very different to her usual activity. 'I only wish I knew what was right,' said Stephen to himself; 'they told us we ought to show respect for father, but I don't think he'd like this. Perhaps if I could read the Bible all through, that would tell me everything.'

This thought reminded Stephen that he had promised his father to read his chapter every day of his life till he knew how to read more; and, carrying the old Bible to his favourite seat on the door-sill, a very pleasant place in the cool, fresh summer morning, he read the verses aloud, slowly and carefully, rather repeating than reading them, for he knew his chapter better by heart than by the printed letters in the book. Thank God, Stephen Fern did begin to know it by heart!

It was not a bad day in the pit. All the colliers, men and boys, were more gentle than usual with the fatherless lad; and even Black Thompson, his master since his father's illness, who was in general a fierce bully to everybody about him, spoke as mildly as he could to Stephen. Yet all the day Stephen longed for his release in the evening, thinking how much work there wanted doing in the garden, and how he and Martha must be busy in it till nightfall. The clanking of the chain which drew him up to the light of day sounded like music to him; but little did he guess that an enemy was lying in wait for him at the mouth of the pit. 'Hillo!' cried a voice down the shaft as they were nearing the top; 'one of you chaps have got to carry a sack o' coals one mile.'

The voice belonged to Tim Cole, who was the terror of the pit-bank, from his love of mischief and his insatiable desire for fighting. He was looking down the shaft now, with a grin and a laugh upon his red face, round which his shaggy red hair hung like a rough mane. There were only two other boys besides Stephen in the skip, and as their fathers were with them it might be dangerous to meddle with them; so Tim fixed upon Stephen as his prey.

'Thee has got to carry these coals, Steve,' he said, his eyes dancing with delight.

'I won't,' replied Stephen.

'Thee shalt,' cried Tim, with an oath.

'I won't,' Stephen repeated stedfastly.

'Then we'll fight for it,' said Tim, clenching his fists and squaring his arms, while the men and boys formed a ring round the two lads, and one and another spoke encouragingly to Stephen, who was somewhat slighter and younger than Tim. He had beaten Tim once before, but that was months ago; yet the blood rushed into Stephen's face, and he set his lips together firmly. Up yonder, just within the range of his sight, was Fern's Hollow, with its neglected garden, and his supper waiting for him; and here was the heavy sack of coals to be carried for a mile, or the choice of fighting with Tim.

'I wish I knew what I ought to do,' he said, speaking aloud, though speaking to himself.

'Ay, ay, lad,' cried Black Thompson; 'it's a shame to make thee fight, and thy father not cold in the graveyard yet. I say, Tim, what is it thee wants?'

'These coals,' answered Tim doggedly, 'are to be carried to the New Farm; and if Stevie Fern won't take them one mile, he must fight me afore he goes off this bank.'

'Now, lads, I'll judge between ye this time,' said Black Thompson. 'Stevie shall carry them to the end of Red Lane, and cut across the hill home: that's not much out of the way; and if Tim makes him go one step farther, I'll lick thee myself to-morrow, lad, I promise thee.'

Stephen hoisted the sack upon his shoulders in silence, and strode away with a swelling heart, in which a tumult of anger and perplexity was raging. 'If I had only a commandment about these things!' he thought. He was not quite certain whether it would not have been best and wisest to fight with Tim and have it out; especially as Tim was all the time taunting him for being a coward. But his father had read much to him during the last three months; and though he could not remember any particular commandment, he felt sure that the Bible did not encourage fighting or drunkenness. Suddenly, and before they reached the end of Red Lane, a light burst upon Stephen's mind.

'I say, Tim,' he said, speaking to him for the first time, 'it's four miles to the New Farm, and I'll go with thee a mile farther than Red Lane.'

'Eh!' cried Tim; 'and get Black Thompson to lick me to-morrow?'

'No,' said Stephen earnestly, 'I'll not tell Black Thompson; and if he hears talk of it, I'll say I did it of my own mind. Come thy ways, Tim; let's be sharp, for I've my potatoes to hoe when I get home to-night.'

The boys walked briskly on for a few minutes, past the end of Red Lane, though Stephen cast a wistful glance up it, and gave an impatient jerk to the load upon his shoulders. Tim had been walking beside him in silent reflection; but at last he came to a sudden halt.

'I can't make it out,' he said. 'What art thee up to, Stephen? Tell me out plain, or I'll fight thee here, if Black Thompson does lick me for it.'

'Why, I've been learning to read,' answered Stephen, with some pride, 'and of course I know things I didn't used to know, and what thee doesn't know now.'

'And what's that to do with it?' inquired Tim.

'My chapter says that if any man forces me to go one mile, I am to go two,' replied Stephen; 'it doesn't say why exactly, but I'm going to try what good it will be to me to do everything that my book tells me.'

'It's a queer book,' said Tim, after a pause. 'Does it say a chap may make another chap do his work for him?'

'No,' Stephen answered; 'but it says we are to love our enemies, and do good to them that hate us, that we may be the children of our Father which is in heaven—that is God, Tim. So that is why I am going a mile farther with thee.'

'I don't hate thee,' said Tim uneasily, 'but I do love fighting; I'd liever thee'd fight than come another mile. Don't thee come any farther, I've been bone lazy all day, and thee's been at work. And I say, Stevie, I'll help thee with the potatoes to-morrow, to make up for this bout.'

Stephen thanked him, and accepted his offer heartily. The load was quickly transferred to Tim's broad back, and the boys parted in more good-will than they had ever felt before; Stephen strengthened by this favourable result in his resolution to put in practice all he knew of the Bible; and Tim deep in thought, as was evident from his muttering every now and then on his way to the New Farm, 'Queer book that; and a queer chap too!'


CHAPTER IV

THREATENING CLOUDS

Little Nan would be waiting for him, as well as his supper, and Stephen forgot his weariness as he bounded along the soft turf, to the great discomfiture of the brown-faced sheep, quite as anxious for their supper as he was for his.

Stephen heard far off Snip's sharp, impatient bark, and it made him quicken his steps still more, until, coming within sight of his own Hollow, he stopped suddenly, and his heart beat even more vehemently than when he was running up the hillside.

There was, however, nothing very terrible in the scene. The hut was safe, and the sun was shining brightly upon the garden, and little Nan was standing as usual at the wicket. Only in the oat-field, with their faces looking across the green, stood two men in close conversation. These men were both of them old, and rather thin and shrivelled in figure; their features bore great resemblance to each other, the eyes being small and sunken, with many wrinkles round them, and both mouths much fallen in. You would have said at once they were brothers; and if you drew near enough to hear their conversation, you would have found your guess was right.

'Brother Thomas,' said the thinnest and sharpest-looking, 'I intend to enclose as far as we can see from this point. That southern bank will be a first-rate place for young animals. I shall build a house, with three rooms above and below, besides a small dairy; and I shall plant a fir-wood behind it to keep off the east winds. The lime and bricks from my own works will not cost me much more than the expense of bringing them up here.'

'And a very pretty little hill-farm you'll make of it, James,' replied Thomas Wyley admiringly. 'I should not wonder now if you got £20 a year rent for it.'

'I shall get £25 in a few years,' said the other one: 'just think of the run for ponies on the hill, to say nothing of sheep. A young, hard-working man could make a very tidy living up here; and we shall have a respectable house, instead of a pauper's family.'

'It will be a benefit to the neighbourhood,' observed Thomas Wyley.

The latter speaker, who was a degree pleasanter-looking than his brother, was the relieving officer of the large union to which Botfield belonged; and, in consequence, all poor persons who had grown too old, or were in any way unable to work, were compelled to apply to him for the help which the laws of our country provide for such cases. James Wyley, the elder brother, was the owner of Botfield works, and the master of all the people employed in them, besides being the agent of the lord of the manor. So both these men possessed great authority over the poor; and they used the power to oppress them and grind them down to the utmost. It was therefore no wonder that Stephen stopped instantly when he saw their well-known figures standing at the corner of his oat-field; nor that he should come on slowly after he had recovered his courage, pondering in his own mind what they were come up to Fern's Hollow for, and how he should answer them if they should want him to give up the old hut.

'Good evening, my lad,' said James Wyley, smiling a slow, reluctant smile, as Stephen drew near to them with his cap in his hand. 'So you buried your father yesterday, I hear. Poor fellow! there was not a better collier at Botfield than James Fern.'

'Never troubled his parish for a sixpence,' added Thomas Wyley.

'Thank you, master,' said Stephen, the tears starting to his eyes, so unexpected was this gentle greeting to him; 'I'll try to be like father.'

'Well, my boy,' said Thomas Wyley, 'we are come up here on purpose to give you our advice, as you are such a mere lad. I've been thinking what can be done for you. There's your grandfather, a poor, simple, helpless old man, and the little girl—why, of course we shall have to receive them into the House; and I'll see there is no difficulty made about it. Then we intend to get your sister into some right good service.'

'I should not mind taking her into my own house,' said the master, Mr. James Wyley; 'she would soon learn under my niece Anne. So you will be set free to get your own living without encumbrance; you are earning your six shillings now, and that will keep you well.'

'Please, sir,' answered Stephen, 'we mean to live all together as we've been used; and I couldn't let grandfather and little Nan come upon the parish. Martha must stay at home to mind them; and I'll work my fingers to the bone for them all, sir. Many thanks all the same to you for coming up here to see after us.'

'Very fine indeed, my little fellow,' said Thomas Wyley; 'but you don't understand what you are talking about. It is my place to see after the poor, and I cannot leave you in charge of such a very old man and such a child as this, No, no; they must be taken care of; and they'll be made right comfortable in the House.'

'Father said,' replied Stephen, 'that I was never to let grandfather and little Nan come upon the parish. I get my wages, and we've no rent to pay; and the potatoes and oats will help us; and Martha can pick bilberries on the hill, and carry bundles of firing to the village; and we'll do well enough without the parish. Many thanks all the same to you, sir.'

'Hark ye, my lad,' said the master impatiently. 'I want to buy your old hut and field from you. I'll give ye a ten-pound note for it; a whole ten pounds. Why, a fortune for you!'

'Father said,' repeated Stephen, 'I was never to give up Fern's Hollow; and I gave him a sure promise for that, and to take care of little Nan as long as ever I lived.'

'Fern's Hollow is none of yours,' cried the master, in a rage; 'you've just been a family of paupers and squatters, living up here by poaching and thieving. I'll unearth you, I promise ye; you have been a disgrace to the manor long enough. So it is ten pounds or nothing for your old hole; and you may take your choice.'

'Please, sir,' said Stephen firmly, 'the place is ours, and I'm never to part with it. I'll never poach, and I'll never trespass on the manor; but I can't sell the old house, sir.'

'Now, just listen to me, young Fern,' said Thomas Wyley; 'you'll be compelled to give up Fern's Hollow in right of the lord of the manor; and then if you come to the House for relief, mark my words, I'll send your grandfather off to Bristol, for that's his parish, and you'll never see him again; and I'll give orders for you never to see little Nan; and I'll apprentice you and your other sister in different places. So you had better be reasonable, and take our advice while you can be made comfortable.'

'Please, sir, I can't go against my promise,' answered Stephen, with a sob.

'What's the use of wasting one's breath?' said the master; 'this place I want, and this place I'll have; and we'll see if this young jail-bird will stand in my way. Ah, my fine fellow, it's no such secret where your grandfather spent twenty-one years of his life; and you'll have a sup of the same broth some day. You don't keep a dog like that yelping cur for nothing; and I'll tell the gamekeeper to have his eye upon you.'

Stephen stood motionless, watching them down the narrow path which led to Botfield, until a rabbit started from beneath the hedge, and Snip, with a sharp, short bark of excitement, gave it chase in the direction of the two men. The master paused, and, looking back, shook his stick threateningly at the motionless figure of the boy; while Thomas Wyley threw a stone at the dog, which sent him back, yelping piteously, to his young master's feet. Stephen clenched his hands, and bit his lips till the blood started, but he did not move till the last glimpse of his foes had passed away from the hillside. Martha had hidden herself in the hut while they were present, for she had never spoken to the dreaded master; but she could overhear their loud and angry speeches, and now she came out and joined Stephen.

'Well, I'd have more spirit than to cry,' she said, as Stephen brushed his eyes with his sleeve; 'I'd never have spoken so gingerly to them, the wizen-faced old rascals. The place is ours, and they can't turn us out. It's no use to be cowed by them, Stephen.'

'They can turn me off the works,' answered Stephen sadly.

'And whatever shall we do then?' asked Martha, in alarm. 'Still I reckon you'll say we are to love those old wretches.'

'The Book says so,' replied Stephen.

'Well, I won't set up to try to do it for one,' continued Martha decisively; 'it's not nature; it's being over good by half. I'm willing to do my duty by you and grandfather and little Nan; but that goes beyond me. If you'd just give way, Stevie, and give them a good rating, you'd feel better after it.'

'I don't know that,' he answered, walking gloomily towards the door. He felt so much passion and anger within him, that it did seem as if it would be a relief to utter some of the terrible oaths which he heard frequently in the pit, and which had been familiar enough in his own mouth a few months ago. But now other words, familiar from daily reading, the words that he had repeated to Tim so short a time before, were being whispered, as it seemed, close by his ear: 'Love your enemies; bless them that curse you; do good to them that hate you; pray for them that despitefully use you, and persecute you.' There was a deadly conflict going on in the boy's soul; and Martha's angry words were helping the tempter. He sat down despondently on the door-sill, and hid his face in his hands, while he listened to his sister's taunts against his want of spirit, and her fears that he would give up their home for his new notions.

He was about to answer her at last with the passion she was trying to provoke, when a soft little cheek was pressed against his downcast head, and little Nan lisped in her broken words, 'Me sleepy, Stevie; me say "Our Father," and go to bed.'

The child knelt down before him, and laid her folded hands upon his knee, as she had done every evening since his father died, while he said the prayer, and she repeated it slowly after him. He felt as though he was praying for himself. A feeling of deep earnestness came over him; and, though his voice faltered as he said softly, 'Forgive us our trespasses, as we forgive them that trespass against us,' it seemed as if there was a spirit in his heart agreeing to the words, and giving him power to say them. He did not know then that 'the Spirit itself maketh intercession for us with groanings which cannot be uttered;' but while he prayed with little Nan, he received great comfort and strength, though he was ignorant of the source from whence they came. When the child's prayers were ended, he roused himself cheerfully to action; and as long as the lingering twilight lasted, both Stephen and Martha were busily at work in the garden.

## CHAPTER V

## MISS ANNE

'So thee's the only master here,' said Tim when he came up the hill next evening, according to his promise, to help Stephen in his garden.

'And I'm the missis,' chimed in Martha, 'but I can't say how long it may be afore we have to pack off;' and she gave Tim a very long account of the master's visit the day before, finishing her description of Stephen's conduct in a tone of mingled reproach and admiration: 'And he never said a single curse at them!'

'Not when they were out of hearing?' exclaimed Tim.

'I couldn't,' answered Stephen; 'I knew what I ought to do then, if I wasn't quite sure about fighting thee, Tim. My chapter says, "Swear not at all;" and "Let your communication be Yea, yea; Nay, nay; for whatsoever is more than these cometh of evil."'

'What's the meaning of that?' asked Tim, opening his eyes widely.

'Father said it meant I was to stand to my word like a man, but not swear about it. If I said Ay, to mean ay; and if I said No, to mean no, and stick to it.'

'There'd be no room for telling lies, I reckon,' said Tim reflectively.

'Of course not,' replied Stephen.

'That 'ud never answer down yonder,' said Tim, nodding towards the distant village. 'I tell thee what, lad, I'll come and quarter with thee, and help thee to be master. It 'ud be prime. Only maybe the victuals wouldn't suit me. Last Sunday, afore thy father's buryin', we'd a dinner of duck and green peas, and leg of lamb, and custard pudden, and ale. Martha doesn't get a dinner like that for thee, I reckon.'

'No,' answered Stephen shortly.

'Maybe it wouldn't suit. But what more is there in thy book?' asked Tim, whose curiosity was aroused; and Stephen, proud of his new accomplishment,—a rare one in those days among his own class,—would not lose the opportunity given him by Tim's inquiry for the display of his learning. He brought out his Bible with alacrity, and read his chapter in a loud, clear, sing-song tone, while Tim overlooked him, with his red face growing redder, and his eyebrows arched in amazement; and Martha, leaning against the door-post, glanced triumphantly at his wonder. Already, though his father had been dead only a week, Stephen began to miscall many of the harder words; but his hearers were not critical, and the performance gave unbounded satisfaction.

'That beats me!' cried Tim. 'What a headpiece thee must have, Stephen! But what does it all mean, lad? Is it all English like?'

'How can I know?' answered Stephen, somewhat sadly; 'there's nobody to learn me now; and it's very hard. There's the Pharisees, Tim, and Raca; I don't know who they are.'

The conversation was stopped by Martha suddenly starting bolt upright, and dropping two or three hurried curtseys. The boys looked up from their book quickly, and saw a young lady passing through the wicket and coming up the garden walk, with a smile upon her pleasant face as she met their gaze.

'My boys,' she said, in a soft, kindly voice, 'I've been sitting on the bank yonder, behind your cottage; and I heard one of you reading a chapter in the Bible. Which of you was it?'

'It was him,' cried Tim and Martha together, pointing at Stephen.

'And you said you had no one to teach you,' continued the lady. 'Now would you learn well, if I promised to teach you?'

Stephen looked up speechlessly into the smiling face before him. He had never read of the angels, and scarcely knew that there were such beings; but he felt as if this fair and sweet-looking lady, with her gentle voice, and the kindly eyes meeting his own, was altogether of a different order to themselves.

'I am Mr. Wyley's niece,' she added, 'and I am come to live at Botfield for a while. Could you manage to come down to Mr. Wyley's house sometimes for a lesson?'

'Please, ma'am,' said Martha, who was not at all afraid of speaking to any lady, though she dare not face the master, 'he wants to turn us out of our house; and he hates Stephen, because he won't give it up: so he wouldn't let you teach him anything.'

'Then you are Stephen Fern?' said the lady; 'I heard my uncle talking about you. Your father was buried at Longville church on Sunday. I saw the funeral leave the churchyard, and I looked for some of you to come in to the evening service. Now, Stephen, do you tell me all about your reason for not letting my uncle buy your cottage.'

Then Stephen, with some hesitation, and a good deal of assistance from Martha, told the whole history of his grandmother's settlement upon the solitary hillside, only withholding the fact of his grandfather's transportation, because Tim was listening eagerly to every word. Miss Anne listened, too, with deep attention; and once or twice the tears rose to her eyes as she heard of the weary labours and watchings of the desolate woman; and when Stephen repeated his resolution to work hard and constantly for the maintenance of his grandfather and little Nan—

'Yes, I will be your friend,' she said, reaching out her hand to him when he had finished, 'even if my uncle is your enemy. God has not given me much power, but what I have I will use for you; and you must go on striving to do right, Stephen.'

'I can't read much,' replied Stephen anxiously, 'and Martha can't read at all; but I hope we shall all get safe to heaven!'

'Knowing how to read will not take us to heaven,' said Miss Anne, smiling, 'but doing the will of God from the heart; and the will of God is that we should believe in the Lord Jesus, and follow in His steps.'

'Yes, ma'am,' answered Stephen; 'my chapter says, "Whosoever shall break one of these least commandments, and shall teach men so, shall be called the least in the kingdom of heaven: but whosoever shall do and teach them, the same shall be called great in the kingdom of heaven."'

'Stephen, you know your chapter well,' said Miss Anne.

'I don't know anything else,' he answered; 'so I am always studying at that in my head, up here and down in the pit.'

'He's always mighty solid over his work, ma'am,' said Tim, pulling the front lock of his red hair, as he spoke to the young lady.

'Stephen, do you know that you have a namesake in the Bible?' asked Miss Anne.

'No, sure!' exclaimed Stephen eagerly.

'It was the name of a man who had many enemies, only because he loved the Lord Jesus; and at last they hated him so much as to kill him. He was the very first person who ever suffered death for the Lord's sake. Give me your Bible, and I will read to you how he died.'

Miss Anne's voice was very low and soft, like sweet music, as she read these verses: 'And they stoned Stephen, calling upon God, and saying, Lord Jesus, receive my spirit. And he kneeled down, and cried with a loud voice, Lord, lay not this sin to their charge. And when he had said this, he fell asleep.'

Stephen listened breathlessly, and his face glowed with intense interest; but he was not a boy of ready speech, and, before he could utter a word, Tim burst in before him with a question, 'Please, is there a Tim in the Bible?' he asked.

'Yes,' answered Miss Anne, smiling again; 'he was a young man who knew the Bible from his youth.'

'That ain't me, however,' said Tim in a despondent tone.

'There is nothing now to prevent you beginning to know it,' continued Miss Anne. 'Listen: as Stephen cannot come to me at Botfield, you shall meet me in the Red Gravel Pit at nine o'clock on a Sunday morning as long as the summer lasts, and I will teach you all. Bring little Nan with you, Stephen.'

Down the same narrow green pathway trodden by the feet of Stephen's angry master and his brother the evening before, they now watched the little light figure of the young lady, as she slowly vanished out of their sight. When the gleaming of her dress was quite lost, Stephen rubbed his eyes for a moment, and then turned to Martha and Tim.

'Is she a real woman, dost think?' he asked.

'A real woman!' repeated Martha rather scornfully; 'of course she is; and it's a real silk gown she had on, I can tell thee. Spirits don't go about in silk gowns and broad daylight, never as I heard tell of, lad.'

# CHAPTER VI

## THE RED GRAVEL PIT

At the entrance of the lane leading down to the works at Botfield there stood a small square building, which was used as the weighing-house for the coal and lime fetched from the pits, and as the pay-office on the reckoning Saturday, which came once a fortnight. Upon the Saturday evening after his interview with the master, Stephen loitered in the lane with a very heavy heart, afraid of facing Mr. Wyley, lest he should receive the sentence of dismissal from the pit. He did not know what he could turn his hand to if he should be discharged from what had been his work since he was eight years old; for even if he could get a place in one of the farmhouses about as waggoner's boy, he would not earn more than three shillings a week; and how very little that would do towards providing food for the three mouths at home! Fearful of knowing the worst, he lingered about the office until all the other workmen had been in and come out again jingling their wages.

But the master and his brother Thomas had been taking counsel together about the matter. Mr. Wyley was for turning the boy off at once, and reducing him to the utmost straits of poverty; but his more prudent brother was opposed to this plan.

'Look here, brother James,' he said; 'if we drive the young scamp to desperation, there's no telling what he will do. Ten to one if he does not go and tell a string of lies to some of the farmers about here, or perhaps to the parson at Longville, and they may make an unpleasant disturbance. Nobody knows and nobody cares about him as it is; but he is a determined young fellow, or I'm mistaken. Better keep him at work under your own eye, and make the place too hot for him by degrees. Before long you will catch him poaching with his dog, and if he is let off for a time or two because of his youth, and goes at it again, we can make out a pretty case of juvenile depravity, without any character from his employer, you know; and so he will be sent out of the way, and boarded at the expense of the country for a few years or so.'

'Well,' said the master, 'I'll try him once again. If he'd go out quietly, nobody else has any claim upon the cottage; and I want to set to work there quickly.'

So when Stephen entered the office with trembling limbs and a very pale face under its dusky covering, it happened that he met with a very different reception to what he expected. The master sat behind a small counter, upon which lay Stephen's twelve shillings, the only little heap of money left; and as he gathered them nervously into his hand, he wondered if this would be the last time. But his master's face was not more threatening than usual; and he muttered his 'Thank you, sir,' and was turning away with a feeling of great relief, when Mr. Wyley's harsh voice brought him back again, trembling more than ever.

'Have you thought any more of my offer, Fern?' he asked. 'I shouldn't mind, as you are an orphan, and have two sisters depending upon you, if I made the ten pounds into fifteen; and you may leave the money at interest with me till you are older.'

'And I've been thinking, Stephen,' added Thomas Wyley, who sat at a high desk checking the accounts, 'that, as you seem set against being separated, instead of taking your grandfather into the House, I'd get him two shillings a week allowed him out of it; and that would pay the rent of a nice two-roomed cottage down in Botfield, close to your work. Come, that would make all of you comfortable.'

'You should bear in mind, Stephen,' said the master, 'that the place does not of right belong to you at all; and the lord of the manor is coming to shoot over the estate in September; and then I shall have orders to remove you by force. So you had better take our offer.'

'Please, sir,' said Stephen, bowing respectfully, 'don't be angered with me, but I can't go from what I said afore. Father told me never to give up Fern's Hollow; and maybe he'd hear tell of it in heaven if I broke my word to him. I can't do it, sir.'

'Well, wilful will have his way,' said Mr. Thomas, nodding at the master; and as neither of them addressed Stephen again, he left the office, amazed to find that he was not forbidden to return to work on the following Monday.

The Red Gravel Pit, where Miss Anne had promised to meet her scholars on Sunday morning, was a quarry cut out of the side of one of the hills, from which the stones were taken for making and mending the roads in the neighbourhood. The quarry had been hollowed out into a kind of enclosed circle, only entered by the road through which the waggons passed. All along the edge of the red rocks high overhead there was a coppice of green hazel-bushes and young oaks, where the boys had spent many a Sunday searching for wild nuts, and hunting the squirrels from tree to tree. Stephen and Tim met half an hour earlier than the time appointed by Miss Anne, and by dint of great perseverance and strength rolled together five large stones, under the shadow of an oak tree; and placed four of them in a row before the largest one, as Tim had once seen the children sitting in the village school at Longville, when he had taken a donkey-load of coals for the schoolmaster. Martha came in good time with little Nan, both in their new black bonnets and clean cotton shawls; and all were seated orderly in a row when Miss Anne entered the Red Gravel Pit by the waggon road.

I need not describe to you how Miss Anne heard Stephen read his chapter, and taught Tim and Martha, and even little Nan herself, the first few letters of the alphabet; after which she made them all repeat a verse of a hymn, and, when they could say it correctly, sang it with them over and over again, in her sweet and clear voice, until Stephen felt almost choked with a sob of pure gladness, that would every now and then rise to his lips. Tim sang loudly and lustily, getting out of tune very often. But little Nan was a marvel to hear, so soft and sweet were her childish tones, so that Miss Anne bade her sing the verse alone, which she did perfectly. Martha, too, was full of admiration of the lady's lilac silk dress and the white ribbon on her bonnet.

That was the first of many pleasant Sunday mornings in the Red Gravel Pit. When the novelty was worn away, Martha discovered that she had too much to do at home to be able to leave it so early in the day; and Tim sometimes overslept himself on a Sunday, when most of his comrades spent the whole morning in bed. But Stephen and little Nan were always there, and their teacher never failed to meet them. Nor did Miss Anne confine her care of the orphan children to a Sunday morning only. Sometimes she would mount the hill during the long summer evenings, and pay their little household a visit, giving Martha many quiet hints about her management and her outlay of Stephen's wages; hints which Martha did not always receive as graciously as they were given. Miss Anne would read also to the blind old grandfather, choosing very simple and easy portions of the Bible, especially about the lost sheep being found, as that pleased the old shepherd, and he could fully understand its meaning. In general, Miss Anne was very cheerful, and she would laugh merrily at times; but now and then her face looked pale and sad, and her voice was very mournful while she talked and sang with them. Once, even, when she bade Stephen 'good evening,' an exceedingly sorrowful expression passed across her face, and she said to him, 'I find it quite as hard work to serve God really and truly as you do, Stephen. There is only one Helper for both of us; and we can only do all things through Christ which strengtheneth us.'

But Stephen could not believe that good, gentle Miss Anne found it as hard to be a Christian as he did. Everything seemed against him at the works. The short indulgence from hard words and hard blows granted him after his father's death was followed by what appeared to be a very tempest of oppression. It was very soon understood that the master had a private grudge against the boy; and though the workpeople were ground down and wronged in a hundred ways by him, so as to fill them with hatred and revenge, they were not the less willing to take advantage of his spite against Stephen. His work underground, which had always been distasteful to him compared with a shepherd's life on the hills, was now made more toilsome and dangerous than ever, while Black Thompson followed him everywhere and all day long with oaths and blows. Stephen's evident superiority over the other boys was of course very much against him; for he had never been much associated with them, as his distant home had separated him from them excepting during the busy hours of labour. Now, when, through his own self-satisfaction and Tim's loud praises, his accomplishments became known, it is no wonder that a storm of envy and jealousy raged round him; for not only the boys themselves, but their fathers also, felt affronted at his wonderful scholarship. To be sure, Tim never deserted him, and his partisanship was especially useful on the bank, before he went down and after he came up from the pit. But below, in the dark, dismal passages of the pit, many a stripe, unmerited, fell upon his bruised shoulders, which he learned to bear the more patiently after Miss Anne had taught and explained to him the verse, 'But He was wounded for our transgressions, He was bruised for our iniquities; the chastisement of our peace was upon Him; and with His stripes we are healed.' Still Stephen, feeling how hard it was to continue in the right way, and knowing how often he failed, to his own sore mortification and the rude triumph of his comrades, wondered exceedingly how it was possible for Miss Anne to find it as hard to be a follower of Christ as he did.


CHAPTER VII

POOR SNIP

The middle weeks of August were come—sunny, sultry weeks; and from the brow of the hill, all the vast plain lying westward for many miles looked golden with the corn ripening for harvest. The oats in the little field had already been reaped; and the fruit in the garden, gathered and sold by Martha, had brought in a few shillings, which were carefully hoarded up to buy winter clothing. It was now the time of the yearly gathering of bilberries on the hills; and tribes of women and children ascended to the tableland from all the villages round. It was the pleasantest work of the year; and Martha, who had never missed the bilberry season since she could remember, was not likely to miss it now. Even little Nan could help to pick the berries, and she and Martha were out on the hillsides all the livelong summer day. Their dwelling on the spot gave them a good advantage over those who lived down in Botfield; and each day, before any of the others could reach the best bilberry-wires, they had already picked a quart of the small purple berries, fresh and cool with the dew of the morning. Only the poor old grandfather had to be left at home alone, with his dinner put ready for him, which he was apt to eat up long before the proper dinner-hour came; and then he had to wait until Stephen returned from his work, or Martha and little Nan were driven home by the August thunderstorms. Martha was wonderfully successful this year, and gained more money by selling her bilberries than she thought necessary to show to Stephen; though, on his part, he always brought her every penny of his wages.

Ever since their father's funeral there had been a subject of dispute between the brother and sister. Martha was bent upon enclosing the green dell, with its clear, cool little pond; and to this end she spent all the time she could spare in raising a rough fence of stones and peat round it. But Stephen would not consent to it; and neither argument, scolding, nor coaxing could turn him. He always answered that he had promised the master that he would not trespass on the manor; and he must stand to his word, whatever they might lose by it; though, indeed, he saw no harm in making green fields out of the waste land. Martha, on her side, maintained her right as the eldest to act as she judged best; and, moreover, urged the example of her thrifty grandmother, who had planned this very enclosure, and whose pattern she was determined to follow. But before long the dispute was ended, and the subject of it became a matter of heart-troubling wonder, for several labourers from the master's farm began to fence in the very same ground, as well as to prepare the turf behind Fern's Hollow for the planting of young trees; and neither Stephen nor Martha could hide from the other that these labours made them feel exceedingly uneasy.

'I say, Stephen,' said one of the hedgers, as he was going down from his work one evening, and met the tired boy coming up from his, 'I'm afeared there's some mischief brewing. There's master, and Mr. Thomas, and Mr. Jones the gamekeeper, been talking with thy grandfather nigh upon an hour. There'll be a upshot some day, I know; and Jones, he said summat about leaving a keepsake for thee.'

'What could it be, William?' asked Stephen anxiously.

'How should I know?' said the man, with some reluctance. 'Only, lad, I did hear a gun go off; and I never heard Snip bark again, though I listened for him. Stephen, Stephen, dunna thee go so mad like!'

But it was no use shouting after Stephen, as he ran frantically up the hill. Snip was always basking lazily in the sunshine under the hedge of the paddock, at the very point where he could catch the first sight of his young master, after which there was no more idleness or stillness in him. Stephen could hardly breathe when he found that Snip was not at the usual place to greet him; but before he reached his home he saw it—the dead body of his own poor Snip—hung on the post of the wicket through which he had to pass. He flew to the place; he tore his own hands with the nails that were driven through Snip's feet; and then, without a thought of his grandfather or of his own hunger, he bore away the dead dog in his arms, and wandered far out of sight or sound of the hateful, cruel world, into one of the most solitary plains upon the uplands.

Any one passing by might have thought that Stephen was fast asleep in the last slanting rays of the sun, which shone upon him there some time after the evening shadows had fallen upon Botfield; but a frenzy of passion, too strong for any words, had felled him to the ground, where he lay beside Snip. The gamekeeper, who had so many dogs that he did not care for any one of them in particular, had killed this one creature that was dearer to him than anything in the world, except little Nan, and grandfather, and Martha. And Snip was dead, without remedy; no power on earth could bring back the departed life. Oh, if he could only punish the villain who had shot his poor faithful dog! But he was nothing but a poor boy, very poor, and very helpless and friendless, and people would only laugh at his trouble. All the world was against him, and he could do nothing to revenge himself, but to hate everybody!

'Why, lad! why, Stephen! what ails thee?' said Black Thompson's voice, close behind him. 'Eh! who's gone and shot Snip? That rascal Jones, I'll go bail! Is he quite dead, Stephen? Stand up, lad, and let's give a look at him.'

The boy rose, and faced Black Thompson and his comrade with eyes that were bloodshot, though he had not shed a tear, and with lips almost bitten through by his angry teeth. Both the men handled the dog gently and carefully, but, after a moment's inspection, Thompson laid it down again on the turf.

'It's a shame!' he cried, with an oath that sounded pleasantly in Stephen's ears; 'it was one of the best little dogs about. I'd take my vengeance on him for this. In thy place, I couldn't sleep till I'd done something.'

'Ay!' said Stephen, with flashing eyes; 'I know where he's keeping a covey of birds up against game day— nineteen of them. I've seen them every day, and I could go to the place in the dark.'

'That's a brave lad!' said Black Thompson; 'he's got his father's pluck after all, as I've always told thee, Davies, and we'll see him righted. He's got his eyes in his head, has this lad!'

'They're down in the leasowe, between the Firspinny and Ragleth Hill,' continued Stephen; 'and they're just prime, I can tell ye. And I know, too, what he doesn't know himself. I know to some black game, far away up the hill. He'd give his two eyes to see them, with their white wing-feathers; and if he hadn't'—

Stephen stopped, with quivering lips, for he could not speak yet of Snip's murder.

'Never take on, my lad,' said Black Thompson, clapping him on the back; 'we'll spoil his sport for him. Come thy ways with us; it'll be dark dusk afore we gain the spinny, and Jones is off to the Whitehurst woods to-night. We'll have as rare sport as the lord of the manor himself. Thee art a sharp one. I'd lay a round wager, now, thee knows where all the sheep of the hillside fold of nights.'

'Ay, do I,' answered Stephen, walking briskly beside Black Thompson; 'I know every walk and every fold on the hills; ay, and many of the sheep themselves. I keep my eyes wide open out of doors, I promise ye.'

'I'll swear to that,' said Black Thompson, glad to encourage the boy in his foolish boasting. On their way they passed near to Fern's Hollow, and Stephen heard little Nan's shrill voice calling his name, as if she were seeking him weariedly; but when he hesitated for a moment, his heart yearning to answer her, Black Thompson again patted him on the back, and bade him never show the white feather, but remember poor dead Snip; at which his passion for revenge returned, and he pressed on eagerly to the fir-coppice.

It was quite dark when they entered the path leading through the wood. No one spoke now, and they trod cautiously, lest there should be any noise from their footsteps. The tall black fir-trees towered above them to an unusual height; and through all the topmost branches there ran a low, mournful sound, as if every tree was whispering about them, and lamenting over them. Even the little brook, which in the sunshine rippled so merrily along the borders of the wood, seemed to be sobbing like a grieved and tired child in the night-time. Strange rustlings on every side, and sudden groanings of the withered boughs in some of the pines, made them start in fear; and once, in a little opening among the trees, when the stars came out and looked down upon them, Stephen would have given all he had in the world to be safe at home, with little Nan singing hymns on his knee, or quietly asleep after the hot and busy day.

'It's lonesome enough to make a bull-dog afeared,' whispered Davies, in a frightened tone. But before long they were out of the wood; and in the glimmer of light that lasts all night through during the summer, Stephen saw Black Thompson unwind a net, which had been wrapped round his body under his collier's jacket. More than half the covey of partridges were bagged; and they had such capital luck, as the men called it, that Stephen soon entered into the daring spirit of the adventure. It sent a thrill of excitement through him, in which poor Snip was for the time forgotten; and when about midnight Black Thompson and Davies said 'Good-night' to him at his cottage door, calling him a brave fellow, and giving him a fine young leveret, with the promise that he should have his share of whatever money they received for their spoil, he entered his dark home, where every one was slumbering peacefully, and, without a thought of sorrow or repentance, was quickly asleep himself.

## CHAPTER VIII

### STEPHEN AND THE GAMEKEEPER

Martha's exclamation of surprise and delight at seeing the leveret was the first sound that Stephen heard in the morning; but he preserved a sullen silence as to his absence the previous night, and Martha was too shrewd to press him with questions. They had not been unused to such fare during their father's lifetime; and it was settled between them that she should come down from the bilberry-plain early in the afternoon to make a feast of the leveret by the time of Stephen's return from the pit.

All day long Stephen found himself treated with marked distinction and favour by Black Thompson and his comrades, to some of whom he heard him say, in a loud whisper, that 'Stephen 'ud show himself a chip of the old block yet.' At dinner they invited him to sit within their circle, where he laughed and talked with the best of them, and was listened to as if he were already a man. How different to his usually hurried meal beside the horses, that worked like himself in the dark, close passages, but did not, like him, ascend each evening to the grassy fields and the pure air of the upper earth! Stephen had a true tenderness in his nature towards these dumb fellow-labourers, and they loved the sound of his voice, and the kindly patting of his hand; but somehow he felt as if they knew how he had left his faithful old Snip unburied on the open hillside, where Black Thompson had found him in his passion the evening before. He was not sorry for what he had done; he would avenge himself on the gamekeeper again whenever there was an opportunity. Even now, he promised Black Thompson, when they were away from the other colliers, to show him the haunts of the scarce black grouse, which would be so valuable to the gamekeeper; and he enjoyed Black Thompson's applause. But there was a sore pang in his heart, as he remembered dead Snip, unburied on the hillside.

Supper was ready when he reached home; and what a savoury smell came through the open door, quite down to the wicket! Of course Snip was not watching for him; and little Nan also, instead of looking out for him as usual, was waiting eagerly to be helped; for, as soon as Stephen was seen over the brow of the hill, Martha poured her dainty stew into a large brown dish, and she had already portioned out a plateful for the grandfather. Few words were uttered, for Martha was hot, and rather testy; and Stephen felt a sullen weight hanging upon his spirits. Only every now and then the old grandfather, chuckling and mumbling over the uncommon delicacy, would call Stephen by his father's name of James, and thank him for his rare supper.

'Good evening,' said Miss Anne's voice, and as the light from the doorway was darkened, all the party looked up quickly, and Stephen felt himself growing hot and cold by turns. 'Your supper smells very nice, Martha; there has been some good cooking done to-day.'

'Oh, Miss Anne,' cried Martha, colouring up with excitement and fear, 'it is a young leveret Mrs. Jones, the gamekeeper's wife, gave me for some knitting I'd done for her; she said it 'ud be a treat for grandfather. I've been cooking it all evening, ma'am, and it's very toothsome. If you'd only just taste a mouthful, it 'ud make me ever so proud.'

'Thank you, Martha,' said Miss Anne, smiling; 'I am quite hungry with climbing the hill, and if it is as good as the bread you gave me the other day, I shall enjoy having my supper with you.'

Stephen scarcely heard what Miss Anne said to him, while he watched Martha bustling about to reach out a grand china plate, which was one of the great treasures of their possessions; and he looked on silently as she chose the daintiest morsels of the stew; but when she moved the little table nearer to the door, and laid the plate and knife and fork upon it, before Miss Anne, he started to his feet, unable to sit still and see her partake of the food which he had procured in such a manner.

'Don't touch it! don't taste it, Miss Anne!' he cried excitedly. 'Oh, please to come out with me to the bent of the hill, and I'll tell you why. But don't eat any of it!'

He darted out at the door before Martha could stop him, and ran down the green path to a place where he was out of sight and hearing of his home, waiting breathlessly for Miss Anne to overtake him. It was some minutes before she came, and her face was overcast and troubled; but she listened in silence, while, without concealment, but with many bitter and passionate words against the gamekeeper, and excuses for his own conduct, he confessed to her all the occurrences of the night before. Every moment his agitation increased under her quiet, mournful look of reproach, until, as he came to the close, he cried out in a sorrowful but defiant tone, 'Oh, Miss Anne, I could not bear it!'

'Do you remember,' she asked, in a low and tender voice, 'how poor Snip used to follow me down to this very spot, and sit here till I was out of sight? I was very fond of poor old Snip, Stephen!' Yes, her voice trembled, and tears were in her eyes. The proud bulwark which Stephen had been raising against his grief was broken down in a moment. He sank down on the turf at Miss Anne's feet; and, no longer checking the tears which had been burning in his eyes all day, he wept and sobbed vehemently, until his passion had worn away.

'And now,' said Miss Anne, sitting down beside him, 'I must tell you that, though I am not surprised, I am very, very grieved, Stephen. If you knew your Bible more, you would have read this verse in it, "God is faithful, who will not suffer you to be tempted above that ye are able; but will with the temptation also make a way to escape, that ye may be able to bear it." Did no way of escape open to you, Stephen?'

Then Stephen remembered how he had heard dear little Nan calling piteously to him as he passed Fern's Hollow with Black Thompson; and how his heart yearned to go to her, though he had resisted and conquered this saving impulse.

'You do not know much,' continued Miss Anne, 'but if you had followed out all you do know, instead of poaching with Black Thompson that you might revenge yourself for Snip being killed, you would have been praying for them that persecute you. The Bible says that not a sparrow falls to the ground without our Father. So God knew that poor Snip was shot.'

'But why did He not hinder it?' asked Stephen, speaking low and indistinctly.

'Stephen,' said Miss Anne earnestly, 'suppose that I lived in a very grand palace, where there were many things that you had never seen, and I wanted little Nan to come and live with me, not as a servant, but as my dear child; would it be unkind of me to send her first to a school, where she could learn how to read the books, and understand the pictures, and play the music she would find in my palace? Even if the lessons were often hard, and some of her schoolfellows were cruel and unkind to her, would it not be better for her to bear it for a little while, until she was made ready to live with me as my own child?'

The young lady paused for a few minutes, while Stephen pictured to himself the grand palace, and little Nan being made fit to live in it; and when at last he raised his brown eyes to hers, bright with the pleasant thought, she went on in a quiet, reverential tone:

'Perhaps we could not understand any of the things of heaven, so our Father which is in heaven sends us to school here; we are learning lessons all our life long. There is not a single trouble that comes to us but it is to teach us the meaning of something we shall meet with there. We should not be happy to hear the angels singing a song which we could not understand, because we had missed our lessons down here.'

'Oh, Miss Anne,' cried Stephen, 'I feel as if I could bear anything when I think of that! Only I wish I was as strong as an angel.'

'Patience is better than strength,' said Miss Anne, in a tone as if she were speaking to herself: 'patiently to bear the will of God, and patiently to keep His commandments, is greater and more glorious than the strength of an angel.'

'Black Thompson was so kind to me all to-day,' said Stephen, sighing; 'and now he'll be ten times worse if I go back from telling him where the black game is.'

'You must do right,' replied Miss Anne, with a glance that brought back true courage to the boy's heart; 'and remember that "blessed are they which are persecuted for righteousness' sake, for theirs is the kingdom of heaven." Now, good-night, Stephen. Go and bury poor Snip while there is daylight, in some quiet place where you can go and think and read and play sometimes.'

Stephen returned to the hut for a spade, and then went, with a strange blending of grief and gladness, to the place where he had left his poor dog. He chose a solitary yew tree on the hill for the burial ground, and dug as deep a grave as he could among the far-spreading roots. It was strange, only such things do happen now and then, that while he was working away hard and fast, with the dead dog lying by under the trunk of the yew tree, the gamekeeper himself passed that way. He had been in a terrible temper all day, for he had discovered the mischief done down in the fir-coppice, and the loss of his carefully-preserved covey. The sight of Stephen and dead Snip irritated him; though a feeling of shame crept over him as he saw how tear-stained the boy's face was.

'Mr. Jones,' said Stephen, 'I've something to say to you.'

'Be sharp, then,' replied the gamekeeper, 'and mind what you're about. I'll not take any impudence from a young rascal like you.'

'It's no impudence,' answered Stephen; 'only I know to some black game, and I wanted to tell you about them.'

'Black game!' he said contemptuously. 'A likely story. There's been none these half-dozen years.'

'It's four years since,' answered Stephen; 'I remember, because grandfather and I saw them the day mother died, when little Nan was born. I couldn't forget them or mistake them after that. They are at the head of the Black Valley, where the quaking noise begins. I'm sure I'm right, sir.'

'You are not making game of me?' asked Jones, laughing heartily at his own wit. 'Well, my lad, if this is true, it will be worth something to me. Hark ye, I'm sorry about your dog, and you shall choose any one of mine you like, if you'll promise to keep him out of mischief.'

'I couldn't have another dog in Snip's place,' replied Stephen in a choked voice; 'at any rate not yet, thank you, sir.'

'Well,' said the gamekeeper, shouldering his gun, and walking off, 'I'll be your friend, young Fern, when it does not hurt myself.'


CHAPTER IX

HOMELESS

Of course Stephen's brief term of favour with Black Thompson was at an end; but whether Miss Anne had given him a hint that the boy was under her protection, and had confessed all to her, or because he might be busy in some deeper scheme of wickedness, he did not display as much anger as Stephen expected, when he refused to show him the haunts of the grouse, or go with him again on a poaching expedition. Stephen was more humble and vigilant than he had been before falling into temptation. He set a close watch upon himself, lest he should be betrayed into a self-confident spirit again; and Tim's loud praises sounded less pleasantly in his ears, so that one evening he told him, with much shame, into what sin he had been led by his desire to avenge Snip's murder. Unfortunately, this disclosure so much heightened Tim's estimation of his character, that from time to time he gave utterance to mysterious hints of the extraordinary courage and spirit Stephen could manifest when occasion required. These praises were, however, in some measure balanced by Martha's taunts and reproaches at home.

The shooting season had commenced, and the lord of the manor was come, with a number of his friends, to shoot over the hills and plantations. He was a frank, pleasant-looking gentleman, but far too grand and high for Stephen to address, though he gazed wistfully at him whenever he chanced to meet him on the hills. One afternoon Martha saw him and the master walking towards Fern's Hollow, where the fencing-in of the green and of the coppice behind the hut were being finished rapidly; and she crept with stealthy steps under the hedge of the garden, until she came within earshot of them; but they were just moving on, and all she heard of the conversation were these words, from the lord of the manor: 'You shall have it at any rate you fix, Wyley—at a peppercorn rent, if you please; but I will not sell a square yard of my land out and out.' How Martha and Stephen did talk about those words over and over again, and could never come to any conclusion about them.

It was about noon on Michaelmas Day, a day which was of no note up at Fern's Hollow, where there was no rent to be paid, and Martha was busily hanging out clothes to dry on the gorse bushes before the house, when she saw a troop of labourers coming over the brow of the hill and crossing the newly-enclosed pasture. They were armed with mattocks and pickaxes; but as the peaceful little cottage rose before them, with blind old Fern basking in the warm sunshine, and little Nan playing quietly about the door-sill, the men gathered into a little knot, and stood still with an irresolute and ashamed aspect.

'They know nothing about it,' said William Morris; 'look at them, as easy and unconcerned as lambs. I was afeared there'd be a upshot, when the master were after old Fern so long. I don't half like the job; and Stephen isn't here. He does look a bit like a man, and we could argy with him; but that old man, and that girl—they'll take on so.'

'I say, Martha,' shouted a bolder-hearted man, 'hasn't the master let thee know thee must turn out to-day? He wants to lay the foundation of a new house, and get the walls up afore the frost comes on; and we are come to pick the old place to the ground. He only told us an hour ago, or we'd have seen thee was ready.'

'I don't believe thee; thee's only romancing,' said Martha, turning very pale. 'The old place is our own, and no master has any right to it, save Stephen.'

'It's no use wasting breath,' replied William Morris. 'The master says he's bought the place from thy grandfather, lass; and he agreed to turn out by noon on Michaelmas Day. Master doesn't want to be hard upon you; and he says, if you've no place to turn in to, you may go to the old cabin on the upper cinder-hill, till there's a cottage empty in Botfield; and we'll help thee to move the things at wunst. We're to get the roof off and the walls down afore nightfall.'

'Grandfather and little Nan!' screamed Martha; 'get into the house this minute! It's no use you men coming up here on this errand. You know grandfather's simple, and he hasn't sold the house; how could he? He's no more sense than little Nan. No, no; you must go down to the works, and hear what Stephen says. You're a pack of rascals, every one of you, and the master's the biggest; and you'll all have to gnash your teeth over this business some day, I reckon.'

By this time the old man and the child were safely within the house; and Martha, springing quickly from the wicket, where she had kept the men at bay, followed them in, and barred the door, before any one of the labourers could thrust his shoulder in to prevent her. They held a consultation together when they found that no arguments prevailed upon her to open to them, to which Martha listened disdainfully through the large chinks, but vouchsafed no answer.

'Come, come, my lass,' said William Morris soothingly; 'it's lost time and strength, thee contending with the master. I don't like the business; but our orders are clear, and we must obey them. Thee let us in, and we'll carry the things down to the cinder-hill cabin for thee. If thee won't open the door, we'll be forced to take the thatch off.'

'I won't,' answered Martha,—'not for the lord of the manor himself. The house is ours, and I 'ware any of you to touch it. Go down to Stephen and hear what he'll say. If thee takes the thatch off, thee shan't move me out.'

But when the old stove-pipe, through which the last breath of the household fire had passed, was drawn up, and the blue sky could be seen through the cloud of dust and dirt with which the hut was filled, choking the helpless old man and the frightened child, Martha's courage failed her; and she went out, with little Nan clinging round her, and spoke as calmly to the invaders as her rising sobs would let her.

'You know it's grandmother's own house,' she said; 'and the lord of the manor himself has no right to it. But I'll go down and fetch Stephen, if you'll only wait.'

'We daren't wait, Martha,' answered Morris kindly; 'and it's no use, lass; the master's too many for thee. But thee go down to Stephen; and we'll move the things safe, as if they were our own, and put them where they'll not be broken; and we'll take care of little Nan and thy poor old grandfather. Tell Stephen we're desperately cut up about it ourselves; but, if we hadn't done it, somebody that has no good-will towards him would have taken the job. So go thy poor ways with thee, my lass; we are main sorry for thee and Stephen.'

The hot, choking smoke from the limekiln was blowing across the works; and the dusty pit-bank was covered with busy men and boys and girls, shouting, laughing, singing, and swearing, when Martha arrived at Botfield. She was rarely seen at the pit, for her thrifty and housewifely habits kept her busy at Fern's Hollow; and the rough, loud voices of the banksmen, the regular beat of the engine, the clanking of chains, and the dust and smoke and heat of the almost strange scene bewildered the hillside girl. She made her way to the cabin, a little hut built near the mouth of the shaft for the use of the people employed about the pit; but before she could see Tim, or fix upon any one to inquire about Stephen from, a girl of her own age, but with a face sunburnt and blackened from her rough and unwomanly work, and in an uncouth dress of sackcloth, which was grimed with coal-dust, came up and peered boldly in her face.

'Why, it's Miss Fern!' she cried, with a loud laugh; 'Miss Fern, Esq., of Fern's Hollow, come to learn us poor pit-folk scholarship and manners. Here, lads! here's Mr. Stephen Fern's fine sister, as knows more nor all of us put together. Give us a bit of your learning, Miss Fern.'

'I know a black-bess when I see one,' replied Martha sharply; and all the boys and girls joined in a ready roar of merriment against Bess Thompson, whose nickname was the common country name for a beetle.

'That'll do!' they shouted; 'she knows a black-bess! Thee's got thy answer, Bess Thompson.'

'What's brought thee to the pit?' asked Bess fiercely; 'we want no scatter-witted hill girls here, I can tell ye. So get off the pit-bank, afore I drive thee off.'

'What's all this hullabaloo?' inquired Tim, making his appearance at the cabin door. 'Why, Martha, what brings thee at the pit? Come in here, and tell me what's up now.'

Tim listened to Martha's tearful story with great amazement and indignation; and, after a few minutes' consideration, he told her he had nothing much to do, and he would get leave to take Stephen's place for the rest of the day, so as to set him free to go home at once. He left her standing in the middle of the cabin, for the rough benches round it looked too black for her to venture to take a seat upon them; and in a short time he shouted to her from a skep, which was being lowered into the pit, promising her that Stephen should come up as soon as possible. It seemed a terribly long time to wait amid that noise and dust, and every now and then Black Bess relieved her feelings by making hideous grimaces at her when she passed the cabin door; but Stephen ascended at last, very stern-looking and silent, for Tim had told him Martha's business; and he hurried her away from the pit-bank before he would listen to the detailed account she was longing to give. Even when they were in the lonely lane leading homewards, and she was talking and sobbing herself out of breath, he walked on without a word passing his lips, though his heart was sending up ceaseless prayers to God for help to bear this trial with patience. Poor old home! There was all the well-used household furniture carried out and heaped together on the turf,—chairs and tables and beds,—looking so differently to what they did when arranged in their proper order. The old man, with his grey head uncovered, was wandering to and fro in sore bewilderment; and little Nan had fallen asleep beside the furniture, with the trace of tears upon her rosy cheeks. But the house was almost gone. The door-sill, where Stephen had so often seen the sun go down as he rested himself from his labours, was already taken up; the old grate, round which they had sat all the winter nights that he had ever known, was pulled out of the rock; and all the floor was open to the mocking sunshine. It is a mournful thing to see one's own home in ruins; and a tear or two made a white channel down the coal-dust on Stephen's cheeks; but he subdued himself, and spoke out to the labourers like a man.

'I know it's not your fault,' he said, as they stood round him, making explanations and excuses; 'but you know grandfather could not sell the place. I'll get you to help me carry the things down to the cinder-hill cabin. The sheep and ponies are coming down the hill, and there'll be rain afore long; and it's not fit for grandfather and little Nan to be out in it. You'll spare time from the work for that?'

'Ay, will we!' cried the men heartily; and, submitting kindly to Stephen's quiet directions, they were soon laden with the household goods, which were scanty and easily removed. Two or three journeys were sufficient to take them all; and when the labourers returned for the last time to their work of destruction, Stephen took little Nan in his arms, and Martha led away the old man; while the sound of the pickaxes and the crash of the rough rubble stones of their old home followed their slow and lingering steps over the new pasture, and down the hillside towards Botfield.

CHAPTER X

THE CABIN ON THE CINDER-HILL

The cinder-hill cabin was situated at the mouth of an old shaft, long out of use, but said to lead into the same pit as that now worked, the entrance to which was about a quarter of a mile distant. The cabin was about the same size as the hut from which the helpless family had been driven; but the thatch wanted so much mending that Stephen and Martha were obliged to draw over it one of their patchwork quilts, to shelter them for the night from the rain which was threatened by the gathering clouds. The door from the hut at Fern's Hollow was fortunately rather too large instead of being too small for the doorway; and William Morris promised to bring them a shutter for the window-place, where there was no glass. Altogether, the cabin was not very inferior to their old home; but, instead of the soft green turf and the fragrant air of the hills, they were surrounded by barren cinder-heaps, upon which nothing would grow but the yellow coltsfoot and a few weeds, and the wind was blowing clouds of smoke from the limekilns over and round the dismal cabin. Stephen, with the profound silence that began to frighten Martha, made every arrangement he could think of for their comfort during the quickly-approaching night; and as soon as this was finished, he washed and dressed himself, as upon a Sunday morning, before going to meet Miss Anne in the Red Gravel Pit. He was leaving the cabin without speaking, when little Nan, who had watched everything in childish bewilderment and dismay, set up a loud, pitiful cry, which he soothed with great difficulty.

'Stevie going to live here?' said the little child at last, with a deep sob.

'Ay, little Nan,' he answered; 'for a bit, darling. Please God, we'll go home again some day. But little Nan shall always live with Stevie. That'll do; won't it?'

'Ay, Stevie,' sobbed the child; and Stephen, kissing her tenderly, put her on to Martha's lap, and walked out into the moonlight. The clouds were hanging heavily in the western sky, but the clearer heavens shone all the brighter by the contrast. The mountains lay before him, calm and immovable in the soft light; and he could see the round outline of his own hollow, at which his heart throbbed for a minute painfully. But there was a hidden corner at the side of the cabin, and there Stephen knelt down to pray earnestly before he went farther on his errand, until, calm and quiet as the hills, and as the moon which seemed to be gazing lovingly upon them, he went on with a brave and stedfast spirit to the master's house.

Botfield Hall was a large, half-timbered farmhouse, with a gabled roof, part of which was made of thatch and the rest of tiles. It stood quite alone, at a little distance from the works, on the other side of them to that where the village was built. The window-casements were framed of stone; and the outer doors were of thick, solid oak, studded with large-headed iron nails. The iron ring that served as a rapper on the back door fell with a loud clang from Stephen's fingers upon the nails, and startled him with its din, so that he could hardly speak to the servant who answered his noisy summons. They crossed a kitchen, into which many doors opened, to a kind of parlour beyond, fitted up with furniture that looked wonderfully handsome and grand in Stephen's eyes, and where the master was sitting by a comfortable fire. The impatient servant pushed him within the door, and closed it behind her, leaving him standing upon a mat, and shyly stroking his cap round and round, while the master sat still, and gazed at him steadily with an assumed air of amazement, though inwardly he was more afraid of the boy than Stephen was of him. It makes a coward of a man or boy to do anybody an injury.

'Pray, what business brings you here, young Fern?' he asked in a gruff voice.

'Sir,' said Stephen firmly, but without any insolence of manner, 'I want to know who has turned us out of our own house. Is it the lord of the manor, or you?'

'I've bought the place for myself,' answered the master, bringing his hand down with a heavy blow upon the table before him, as if he would like to knock Stephen down with the same force.

'There's nobody to sell it but me,' said the boy.

'You think so, my lad, do you? Why, if it were your own, you would have no power over it till you are one-and-twenty. But the place was your grandfather's, and he has sold it to me for £15. When your grandfather returned from transportation his wife's hut became his; and his right to it does not go over to anybody else till he is dead. It never belonged to your father; and you can have no right to it. If you want to see the deed of purchase, it is safe here, witnessed by my brother Thomas and Jones the gamekeeper, and your grandfather's mark put to it. I would show it to you; but I reckon, with all your learning, you would not make much out of it.'

'Sir,' said Stephen, trembling, 'grandfather is quite simple and dark. He couldn't understand that you were buying the place of him. Besides, he's never had the money?'

'What do you mean, you young scoundrel?' cried the master. 'I gave it into his own hands, and made him put it into his waistcoat pocket for safety. Simple is he, and dark? He could attend his son's funeral four miles off only a few months ago; and he can understand my niece Anne's fine reading, which I cannot understand myself. Ask him for the three five-pound notes I gave him, if you have not had them already.'

'How long ago is it?' inquired Stephen.

'You can't remember!' said the master, laughing: 'well, well, Jones left you a keepsake at your garden wicket for you to remember the day by.'

Stephen's face flushed into a wrathful crimson, but he did not speak; and in a minute or two the master said sharply,—

'Come, be off with you, if you've got nothing else to say.'

'I have got something else to say,' answered Stephen, walking up to the table and looking steadily into his master's face. 'God sees both of us; and He knows you have no right to the place, and I have. I believe some day we'll go back again, though you have pulled the old house down to the ground. I don't want to make God angry with me. But the Bible says He seeth in secret, and He will reward us openly.'

The master shrank and turned pale before the keen, composed gaze of the boy and his manly bearing; but Stephen's heart began to fail him, and, with trembling limbs and eyes that could scarcely see, he made his way out of the room, and out of the house, down to the end of the shrubbery. There he could bear up no longer, and he sat down under the laurels, shivering with a feeling of despair. The worst was come upon him now, and he saw no helper.

'My poor boy,' said Miss Anne's gentle voice, and he felt her hand laid softly on his shoulder. 'My poor Stephen, I have heard all, and I know how bitterly hard it is to bear.'

Stephen answered her only with a low, half-suppressed groan; and then he sat speechless and motionless, as if his despair had completely paralyzed him.

'Listen, Stephen,' she continued, with energy: 'you told me once that the clergyman at Danesford has some paper belonging to you, about the cottage. You must go to him, and tell him frankly your whole story. I do not believe that what my uncle has done would stand in law, and I myself, if it be necessary, would testify that your grandfather could not understand such a transaction. But perhaps it could be settled without going to law, if the clergyman at Danesford would take it in hand; for my uncle is very wishful to keep a good name in the country. But if not, Stephen Fern, I promise you faithfully that should Fern's Hollow ever come into my possession, and I be my uncle's only relative, I will restore it to you as your rightful inheritance.'

She spoke so gravely, yet cheeringly, that a bright hope beamed into Stephen's mind; and when Miss Anne held out her hand to him, as a pledge of her promise, she felt a warm tear fall upon it. He rose up from the ground now, and stood out into the moonlight before her, looking up into her pale face.

'Stephen,' she said, more solemnly than before, 'do you find it possible to endure this injury and temptation?'

'I've been praying for the master,' answered Stephen; but there was a tone of bitterness in his voice, and his face grew gloomy again.

'He is a very miserable man,' said Miss Anne, sighing; 'I often hear him walking up and down his room, and crying aloud in the night-time for God to have mercy upon him; but he is a slave to the love of riches. Years ago he might have broken through his chain, but he hugged it closely, and now it presses upon him very hardly. All his love has been given to money, till he cannot feel any love to God; and he knows that in a few years he must leave all he loves for ever, and go into eternity without it. He will have no rest to-night because of the injury he has done you. He is a very wretched man, Stephen.'

'I wouldn't change with him for all his money,' said Stephen pityingly.

'Stephen,' continued Miss Anne, 'you say you pray for my uncle, and I believe you do; but do you never feel a kind of spite and hatred against him in your very prayers? Have you never seemed to enjoy telling our Father how very evil he is?'

'Yes,' said the boy, hanging down his head, and wondering how Miss Anne could possibly know that.

'Ah, Stephen,' she continued, 'God requires of us something more than such prayers. He bids us really and truly to love our enemies—love which He only can know of, because it is He who seeth in secret and into the inmost secrets of our hearts. I may hear you pray for your enemies, and see you try to do them good; but He alone can tell whether of a truth you love them.'

'I cannot love them as I love you and little Nan,' replied Stephen.

'Not with the same kind of love,' said Miss Anne; 'in us there is something for your love to take hold of and feed upon. "But if ye love them which love you, what reward have ye? do not even the publicans the same?" Your affection for us is the kind that sinners can feel; it is of this earth, and is earthly. But to love our enemies is heavenly; it is Christ-like, for He died for us while we were yet sinners. Will you try to do more than pray for my uncle and Black Thompson? Will you try to love them. Will you try for Christ's sake?'

'Oh, Miss Anne, how can I?' he asked.

'It may not be all at once,' she answered tenderly; 'but if you ask God to help you, His Holy Spirit will work within you. Only set this before you as your aim, and resist every other feeling that will creep in; remembering that the Lord Jesus Himself, who died for us, said to us, "Love your enemies." He can feel for you, for "He was tempted in all points as we are."'

As she spoke the last words, they heard the master's voice calling loudly for Miss Anne, and Stephen watched her run swiftly up the shrubbery and disappear through the door. There was a great bolting and locking and barring to be heard within, for it was rumoured that Mr. Wyley kept large sums of money in his house, and no place in the whole country-side was more securely fastened up by day or night. But Stephen thought of him pacing up and down his room through the sleepless night, praying God to have mercy upon him, yet not willing to give up his sin; and as he turned away to the poor little cabin on the cinder-hill, there was more pity than revenge in the boy's heart.


CHAPTER XI

STEPHEN AND THE RECTOR

The report of the expulsion of the family from Fern's Hollow spread through Botfield before morning; and Stephen found an eager cluster of men, as well as boys and girls, awaiting his appearance on the pit-bank. There was the steady step and glance of a man about him when he came—a grave, reserved air, which had an effect upon even the rough colliers. Black Thompson came forward to shake hands with him, and his example was followed by many of the others, with hearty expressions of sympathy and attempts at consolation.

'It'll be put right some day,' said Stephen; and that was all they could provoke him to utter. He went down to his work; and, though now and then the recollection thrilled through him that there was no pleasant Fern's Hollow for him to return to in the evening, none of his comrades could betray him into any expression of resentment against his oppressor.

In the meantime Miss Anne did not forget to visit the cabin, and cheer, as well as she could, the trouble of poor Martha, whose good and proud housewifery had kept Fern's Hollow cleaner and tidier than any of the cottages at Botfield. It was no easy matter to rouse Martha to take any interest in the miserable cabin where the household furniture had been hastily heaped in the night before; but when her heart warmed to the work, in which Miss Anne was taking an active part, she began to feel something like pleasure in making the new home like the old one, as far as the interior went. Out of doors, no improvement could be made until soil could be carried up the barren and steep bank, to make a little plot of garden ground. But within, the work went on so heartily that, when Stephen returned from the pit, half an hour earlier than usual,—for he had no long walk of two miles now,—he found his grandfather settled in the chimney corner, apparently unconscious of any removal, while both Martha and little Nan seemed in some measure reconciled to their change of dwelling. Moreover, Miss Anne was waiting to greet him kindly.

'Stephen,' she said, 'Martha has found the three notes in your grandfather's pocket all safe. You had better take them with you to the clergyman at Danesford, and do what he advises you with them. And now you are come to live at Botfield, you can manage to go to church every Sunday; even little Nan can go; and there is a night-school at Longville, where you can learn to write as well as read. It will not be all loss, my boy.'

The opportunity for going to Danesford was not long in coming, for Black Thompson and Cole, who were the chief colliers in the pit, chose to take a 'play-day' with the rest of their comrades; and the boys and girls employed at the works were obliged to play also, though it involved the forfeiture of their day's wages—always a serious loss to Stephen. This time, however, he heard the news gladly; and, carefully securing the three notes by pinning them inside his pocket, he set out for his ten miles walk across the tableland to the other side of the mountains, where Danesford lay. His nearest way led straight by Fern's Hollow, and he saw that already upon the old site the foundation was laid for a new house containing three rooms. In everything else the aspect of the place remained unchanged; there still hung the creaking wicket, where little Nan had been wont to look for his coming home, until she could run with outstretched arms to meet him. The beehives stood yet beneath the hedge, and the bees were flying to and fro, seeking out the few flowers of the autumn upon the hillside. The fern upon the uplands, just behind the hollow, was beginning to die, and its rich red-brown hue showed that it was ready to be cut and carried away for fodder; but a squatter from some other hill-hut had trespassed upon Stephen's old domain. Except this one man, the whole tableland was deserted; and so silent was it that the rustle of his own feet through the fading ferns sounded like other footsteps following him closely. The sheep were not yet driven down into the valleys, and they and the wild ponies stood and stared boldly at the solitary boy, without fleeing from his path, as if they had long since forgotten how the bilberry gatherers had delighted in frightening them. Stephen was too grave and manlike to startle them into memory of it, and he plodded on mile after mile with the three notes in his pocket and his hand closed upon them, pondering deeply with what words he should speak to the unknown clergyman at Danesford.

When he reached Danesford, he found it a very quiet, sleepy little village, with a gleaming river flowing through it placidly, and such respectable houses and small clean cottages as put to shame the dwellings at Botfield. So early was it yet, that the village children were only just going to school; and the biggest boy turned back with Stephen to the gate of the Rectory. Stephen had never seen so large and grand a mansion, standing far back from the road, in a park, through which ran a carriage drive up to a magnificent portico. He stole shyly along a narrow side path to the back door, and even there was afraid of knocking; but when his low single rap was answered by a good-tempered-looking girl, not much older than Martha, his courage revived, and he asked, in a straightforward and steady manner, if he could see the parson. At which the servant laughed a little, and, after inquiring his name, said she would see if Mr. Lockwood could spare time to speak to him.

Before long the girl returned, and led Stephen through many winding and twisting passages, more puzzling than the roads in the pit, to a large, grand room, with windows down to the ground, and looking out upon a beautiful flower-garden. It was like the palace Miss Anne had spoken of, for he could not understand half the things that were in the room; only he saw a fire burning in a low grate, the bars of which shone like silver, and upon the carpeted hearth beside it was a sofa, where a young lady was lying, and near to it was a breakfast-table, at which an elderly gentleman was seated alone. He was a very keen, shrewd-looking man, and very pleasant to look at when he smiled; and he smiled upon Stephen, as he stood awe-struck and speechless at his own daring in coming to speak to such a gentleman, and in such a place as this.

'So you are Stephen Fern, of Fern's Hollow,' said Mr. Lockwood; 'I remember christening you, and giving you my own name, thirteen or fourteen years since, isn't it? Your mother had been my faithful servant for several years; and she brought you all across the hills to Danesford to be christened. Is she well—my good Sarah Moore?'

'Mother died four years ago, sir,' murmured Stephen, unable to say any more.

'Poor boy!' said the young lady on the sofa. 'Father, is there anything we can do for him?'

'That is what I am going to hear, my child,' replied Mr. Lockwood. 'Stephen has not come over the hills without some errand. Now, my boy, speak out plainly and boldly, and let me hear what has brought you to your mother's old master.'

Thus encouraged, Stephen, with the utmost simplicity and frankness, though with fewer words than Martha would have put into the narrative, told Mr. Lockwood the whole history of his life; to which the clergyman listened with ever-increasing interest, as he noticed how the boy was telling all the truth, and nothing but the truth, even to his joining Black Thompson in poaching. When he had finished, Mr. Lockwood went to a large cabinet in the room, and, bringing out a bundle of old yellow documents, soon found among them the paper James Fern had spoken of on his death-bed. It was written by the clergyman living in Longville at the time of old Martha Fern's death, to certify that she had settled, and maintained her settlement on the hillside, without paying rent, or having her fences destroyed, for upwards of twenty years, and that the land was her own by the usages of the common.

'I don't know what use it will be,' said Mr. Lockwood, 'but I will take legal advice upon it; that is, I will tell my lawyer all about it, and see what we had best do. You may leave the case in my hands, Stephen. But to-morrow morning we start for the south of France, where my daughter must live all the winter for the benefit of the warm climate; and I must go with her, for she is my only treasure now. Can you live in your cabin till we come home? Will you trust yourself to me, Stephen? I will not see a son of my old servant wronged.'

'Please, sir,' said Stephen, 'the cabin is good enough for us, and we are nearer church and the night-school; only I didn't like to break my word to father, besides losing the old home: we can stay all winter well. I'll trust you, sir; but my work is dangersome, and please God I should get killed, will you do the same for Martha and little Nan?'

'Ay!' answered Mr. Lockwood, coughing down his emotion at the young boy's forethought and care for his sisters. 'If it pleases God, my boy, you will live to make a right good, true-hearted Christian man; but if He should take you home before me, I'll befriend your sisters as long as I live. I like your Miss Anne, Stephen; but your master is a terrible rascal, I fear.'

'Yes, sir,' said Stephen quietly.

'You don't say much about him, however,' replied Mr. Lockwood, smiling at his few words.

'Please, sir, I am trying to love my enemies,' he answered, with a feeling of shyness; 'if I was to call him a rascal, or any other bad word, it 'ud throw me back like, and it's very hard work anyhow. I feel as if I'd like to do it sometimes.'

'You are right, Stephen,' said Mr. Lockwood; 'you are wise in keeping your tongue from evil speaking: for "therewith bless we God, even the Father; and therewith curse we men, which are made after the similitude of God. Out of the same mouth proceedeth blessing and cursing." You have taught an old parson a lesson, my boy. You had better leave your money with me until my lawyer gives us his opinion. Now go home in peace, and serve your master faithfully; but if you should need a friend before I return, come here and ask for the clergyman who is going to take my duty. I will tell him about you, and he will help you until I come home.'

That afternoon Stephen retraced his lonely path across the hills in great gladness of heart; and when he came to Fern's Hollow, he leaped lightly down the bank against which the old stove-pipe had been reared as a chimney, and stood again on the site of the old hearth, in the midst of the new walls of red bricks that were being built up. How the master could remove the new house and restore the old hut was a question of some perplexity to him; but his confidence in the parson at Danesford was so perfect, that he did not doubt for a moment that he could call Fern's Hollow his own again next spring.

## CHAPTER XII

### VISIT OF BLACK BESS

Everybody at Botfield was astonished at the change in Stephen's manner; so cheerful was he, and light-hearted, as if his brief manhood had passed away, with its burden of cares and anxieties, and his boyish freedom and gladsomeness had come back again. The secret cause remained undiscovered; for Martha, fluent in tongue as she was, had enough discretion to keep her own counsel, and seal up her lips as close as wax, when it was necessary. The people puzzled themselves in vain; and Black Thompson left off hinting at revenge to Stephen. Even the master, when the boy passed him with a respectful bow, in which there was nothing of resentment or sullenness, wondered how he could so soon forget the great injury he had suffered. Mr. Wyley would have been better satisfied if the whole family could have been driven out of the neighbourhood; but there was no knowing what ugly rumours and inquiries might be set afloat, if the boy went telling his tale to nobody knows whom.

Upon the whole, Martha did not very much regret her change of dwelling, though she made a great virtue of her patience in submitting quietly to it. To be sure, the cinder-hill was unsightly, and the cabin blackened with smoke; and it was necessary to lock little Nan and grandfather safely within the house whenever she went out, lest they should get to the mouth of the open shaft, where Stephen often amused the child by throwing stones down it, and listening to their rebound against the sides. But still Martha had near neighbours; and until now she had hardly even tasted the luxury of a thorough gossip, which she could enjoy in any one of the cottages throughout Botfield. Moreover, she could get work for herself on three days in the week, to help a washerwoman, who gave her ninepence a day, besides letting little Nan go with her, and have, as she said, 'the run of her teeth.' She had her admirers, too—young collier lads, who told her truly enough she was the cleanest, neatest, tidiest lass in all Botfield. So Martha Fern regarded their residence on the cinder-hill with more complacency than could have been expected. The only circumstance which in her secret heart she considered a serious drawback was her very near neighbourhood to Miss Anne.

'Stephen,' said Martha one Saturday night, after their work was done, 'I've been thinking how it's only thee that's trying to keep the commandments. I'm not such a scholar as thee; but I've heard thy chapter read till it's in my head, as well as if I could read it off book myself. So I'm thinking I ought to love my enemies as well as thee; and I've asked Black Bess to come and have a cup of tea with us to-morrow.'

'Black Bess!' exclaimed Stephen, with a feeling of some displeasure.

'Ah,' said Martha, 'she's always calling me—a shame to be heard. But I've quite forgiven her; and to-morrow I'll let her see I can make pikelets as well as her mother; and we'll have out the three china cups; only grandfather and little Nan must have common ones. I thought I'd better tell thee; and then thee'lt make haste home from church in the afternoon.'

'Black Bess isn't a good friend for thee,' answered Stephen, who was better acquainted with the pit-girl's character than was Martha, and felt troubled at the idea of any companionship between them.

'But we are to love our enemies,' persisted Martha, 'and do good to them that hate us. At any rate I asked her, and she said she'd come.'

'I don't think it means we are to ask our enemies to tea,' said Stephen, in perplexity. 'If she was badly off, like, and in want of a meal's meat, it 'ud be another thing; I'd do it gladly. And on a Sunday too! Oh, Martha, it doesn't seem right.'

'Oh, nothing's right that I do!' replied Martha pettishly; 'thee'rt afraid I'll get as good as thee, and then thee cannot crow over me. But I'll not spend a farthing of thy money, depend upon it. I'm not without some shillings of my own, I reckon. Thee should let me love my enemies as well as thee, I think; but thee'lt want to go up to heaven alone next.'

Stephen said no more, though Martha continued talking peevishly about Black Bess. She was not at all satisfied in her own mind that she was doing right; but Bess had met her at a neighbour's house, where she was boasting of her skill in making pikelets, and she had been drawn out by her sneers and mocking to give her a kind of challenge to come and taste them. She wanted now to make herself and Stephen believe that she was doing it out of love and forgiveness towards poor Bess; but she could not succeed in the deception. All the Sunday morning she was bustling about, and sadly chafing the grandfather by making him move hither and thither out of the way. It was quite a new experience to have any one coming to tea; and all her hospitable and housekeeping feelings were greatly excited by the approaching event.

When Stephen, with tired little Nan riding on his shoulder, returned from church in the afternoon, they found Bess had arrived, and was sitting in the warmest corner, close to a very large and blazing fire, which filled the cabin with light and heat. Bess had dressed herself up in her best attire, in a bright red stuff gown, and with yellow ribbons tied in her hair, which had been brought to a degree of smoothness wonderful to Stephen, who saw her daily on the pit-bank. She had washed her face and hands with so much care as to leave broad stripes of grime round her neck and wrists, partly concealed by a necklace and bracelets of glass beads; and her green apron was marvellously braided in a large pattern. Martha, in her clean print dress, and white handkerchief pinned round her throat, was a pleasant contrast to the tawdry girl, who looked wildly at Stephen as he entered, as if she scarcely knew what to do.

'Good evening, Bess,' he said, as pleasantly as he could. 'Martha told me thee was coming to eat some pikelets with her, so I asked Tim to come too; and after tea we'll have some rare singing. I often hear thee on the bank, Bess, and thee has a good voice.'

Bess coloured with pleasure, and evidently tried her best to be amiable and well-mannered, sitting up nearer and nearer to the fire until her face shone as red as her dress with the heat. Martha moved triumphantly about the house, setting the tea-table, upon which she placed the three china cups, with a gratified glance at the undisguised admiration of Bess; though three common ones had to be laid beside them, for, as Tim was coming, Stephen must fare like grandfather and little Nan. As soon as Tim arrived, she was very busy beating up the batter for the pikelets, and then baking them over the fire; and very soon the little party were sitting down to their feast—Bess declaring politely, between each piece pressed upon her by Martha, that she had never tasted such pikelets, never!

At last, when tea was quite finished, and the table carefully lifted back to a safe corner at the foot of the bed, though Martha prudently replaced the china cups in the cupboard, Tim and Stephen drew up their stools to the front of the fire, and a significant glance passed between them.

'Now then, Stevie,' said Tim, 'thee learn me the new hymn Miss Anne sings with us; and let's teach Bess to sing too.'

Bess looked round uneasily, as if she found herself caught in a trap; but, as Tim burst off loudly into a hymn tune, in which Stephen joined at the top of his voice, she had no time to make any objection. Martha and the old grandfather, who had been a capital singer in his day, began to help; and little Nan mingled her sweet, clear, childish notes with their stronger tones. It was a long hymn, and, before it was finished, Bess found herself shyly humming away to the tune, almost as if it had been the chorus of one of the pit-bank songs. They sang more and more, until she joined in boldly, and whispered to Martha that she wished she knew the words, so as to sing with them. But the crowning pleasure of the evening was when little Nan, sitting on Stephen's knee, with his fingers stroking her curly hair, sang by herself a new hymn for little children, which Miss Anne had been teaching her. She could not say the words very plainly, but her voice was sweet, and she looked so lovely with her tiny hands softly folded, and her eyes lifted up steadily to Stephen's face, that at last Black Bess burst out into a loud and long fit of crying, and wept so bitterly that none of them could comfort her, until the little child herself, who had been afraid of her before, climbed upon her lap and laid her arms round her neck. She looked up then, and wiped the tears from her face with the corner of her fine apron.

'I had a sister once, just like little Nan,' she said, with a sob, 'and she minded me of her. Miss Anne told me she was singing somewhere among the angels, and I thought she'd look like little Nan. But I'm afraid I shall never go where she is; I'm so bad.'

'We'll teach thee how to be good,' answered Martha. 'Thee come to me, Bess, and I'll teach thee the hymns, and the singing, and how to make pikelets, and keep the house clean on a week-day. I'm going to love my enemies, and do good to them that hate me; so don't thee be shy-like. We'll be friends like Stephen and Tim; and weren't they enemies afore Stephen learned to read?'

That night, as Stephen lay down to sleep, he said to himself, 'I'm glad Black Bess came to eat pikelets with Martha. My chapter says, "Whosoever shall do the commandments, and teach them, the same shall be called great in the kingdom of heaven." Perhaps Martha and me will be called great in heaven, if we teach Bess how to do God's commandments.'


CHAPTER XIII

THE OLD SHAFT

Black Bess began to visit the cinder-hill cabin very often. But there was a fatal mistake, which poor Stephen, in his simplicity and single-heartedness, was a long time in discovering. Martha herself had not truly set out on the path of obedience to God's commandments; and it was not possible that she could teach Bess how to keep them. A Christian cannot be like a finger-post, which only points the way to a place, but never goes there itself. She could teach Bess the words of the hymn, and the tunes they were sung to; but she could tell her nothing of the feeling of praise and love to the Saviour with which Stephen sang them, and out of which all true obedience must flow. With her lips she could say, 'Blessed are the poor in spirit,' and 'Blessed are the meek,' and 'Blessed are they that do hunger and thirst after righteousness;' but she cared for none of these things, and felt none of their blessedness in her own soul; and Bess very quickly found out that she would far rather talk about other matters. And because our hearts, which are foolish, and deceitful above all things, and desperately wicked, soon grow weary of good, but are ever ready to delight in evil, it came to pass that, instead of Martha teaching poor ignorant Bess how to do God's will, Bess was leading her into all sorts of folly and wickedness.

It would be no very easy task to describe how unhappy Stephen was when, from day to day, he saw Martha's pleasant sisterly ways change into a rude and careless harshness, and her thrifty, cleanly habits give place to the dirty extravagance of the collier-folk at Botfield. But who could tell how he suffered in his warm, tender-hearted nature, when he came home at night, and found the poor old grandfather neglected, and left desolate in his blindness; and little Nan herself severely punished by Martha's unkindness and quick temper? Not that Martha became bad suddenly, or was always unkind and neglectful; there were times when she was her old self again, when she would listen patiently enough to Stephen's remonstrances and Miss Anne's gentle teaching; but yet Stephen could never feel sure, when he was at his dismal toil underground, that all things were going on right in his home overhead. Often and often, as he looked up to Fern's Hollow, where the new red-brick house was now to be seen plainly, like a city set on a hill, he longed to be back again, and counted the months and weeks until the spring should bring home the good clergyman to Danesford.

One day, during the time allowed to the pit-girls for eating their dinner, Bess came running over the cinderhills in breathless haste to the old cabin. Martha had been busy all the morning, and was still standing at the washing-tub; but she was glad of an excuse for resting herself, and when Bess sprang over the door-sill, she received her very cordially.

'Martha! Martha!' cried Bess; 'come away quickly. Here's Andrew the packman in the lane, with such shawls, Martha! Blue and red and yellow and green! Only five shillings a-piece; and thee canst pay him a shilling a week. Come along, and be sharp with thee.'

'I've got no money to spend,' said Martha sullenly. 'Stephen ought to let grandfather go into the House, and then we shouldn't be so pinched. What with buying for him and little Nan, I've hardly a brass farthing in the world for myself.'

'I'd not pinch,' Bess answered; 'let Stephen pinch if he will. Why, all the lads in Botfield are making a mock at thee, calling thee an old-fashioned piece and Granny Fern. But come and look, anyhow; Andrew will be gone directly.'

Bess dragged Martha by the arm to the top of the cinder-hill, where they could see the pit-girls clustering round the packman in the lane. The black linen wrapper in which his pack was carried was stretched along the hedge, and upon it was spread a great show of bright-coloured shawls and dresses, and the girls were flitting from one to another, closely examining their quality; while Andrew's wife walked up and down, exhibiting each shawl by turns upon her shoulders. The temptation was too strong for Martha; she wiped the soap-suds from her arms upon her apron, and ran as eagerly down to the lane as Black Bess herself.

'Eh! here's a clean, tight lass for you!' cried Andrew, comparing Martha with the begrimed pit-girls about him. 'The best shawl in my pack isn't good enough for you, my dear. Pick and choose. Just make your own choice, and I'll accommodate you about the price.'

'I've got no money,' said Martha.

'Oh, you and me'll not quarrel about money,' replied Andrew; 'you make your choice, and I'll wait your time. I'm coming my rounds pretty regular, and you can put up a shilling or two agen I come, without letting on to father. But maybe you're married, my dear?'

'No,' she answered, blushing.

'It's not far off, I'll be bound,' he continued, 'and with a shawl like this, now, you'd look like a full-blown rose. Come, I'll not be hard upon you, as it's the first time you've dealt with me. That shawl's worth ten shillings if it's worth a farthing, and I'll let you have it for seven shillings and sixpence; half a crown down, and a shilling a fortnight till it's paid up.'

Andrew threw the shawl over her shoulders, and turned her round to the envying view of the assembled girls, who were not allowed to touch any of his goods with their soiled hands. Martha softly stroked the bright blue border, and felt its texture between her fingers; while she deliberated within herself whether she could not buy it from the fund procured by the bilberry picking in the autumn. As Stephen had never known the full amount, she could withdraw the half-crown without his knowledge, and the sixpence a week she could save out of her own earnings. In ten minutes, while Andrew was bargaining with some of the others, she came to the conclusion that she could not possibly do any longer without a new shawl; so, telling the packman that she would be back again directly, she ran as swiftly as she could over the cinder-hill homewards.

In her hurry to accompany Bess to the lane, she had left her cabin door unfastened, never thinking of the danger of the open pit to her blind grandfather and the child. Little Nan had been wearying all morning for a run in the wintry sunshine, out of the close steam of washing in the small hut; but Martha had not dared to let her run about alone, as she had been used to do at Fern's Hollow, in their safe garden. After Martha and Black Bess had left her, the child stood looking wistfully through the open door for some time; but at last she ventured over the door-sill, and her tiny feet painfully climbed the frozen bank behind the house, whence she could see the group of girls in the lane below. Perhaps she would have found her way down to them, but Martha had been cross with her all the morning, and the child's little spirit was frightened with her scolding. She turned back to the cabin, sobbing, for the north wind blew coldly upon her; and then she must have caught sight of the shaft, where Stephen had been throwing stones down for her the night before, without a thought of the little one trying to pursue the dangerous game alone. As Martha came over the cinder-hill, her eyes fell upon little Nan, rosy, laughing, screaming with delight as her tiny hands lifted a large stone high above her curly head, while she bent over the unguarded margin of the pit. But before Martha could move in her agony of terror, the heavy stone dropped from her small fingers, and Nan, little Nan, with her rosy, laughing face, had fallen after it.

Martha never forgot that moment. As if with a sudden awaking of memory, there flashed across her mind all the child's simple, winning ways. She seemed to see her dying mother again, laying the helpless baby in her arms, and bidding her to be a mother to it. She heard her father's last charge to take care of little Nan, when he also was passing away. Her own wicked carelessness and neglect, Stephen's terrible sorrow if little Nan should be dead, all the woeful consequences of her fault, were stamped upon her heart with a sudden and very bitter stroke. Those who were watching her from the lane saw her stand as if transfixed for a moment; and then a piercing scream, which made every one within hearing start with terror, rang through the frosty air, as Martha sprang forward to the mouth of the old pit, and, peering down its dark and narrow depths, could just discern a little white figure lying motionless at the bottom of the shaft.

## CHAPTER XIV

## A BROTHER'S GRIEF

In a very short time all the people at work on the surface of the mine knew that Stephen Fern's little sister was dead—lying dead in the very pit where he was then labouring for her, with the spirit and strength and love of a father rather than a brother. Every face was overcast and grave; and many of the boys and girls were weeping, for little Nan had endeared herself to them all since she came to live at the cinder-hill cabin. Tim felt faint and heart-sick, almost wishing he could have perished in the child's stead, for poor Stephen's sake; but he had to rouse himself, for one of the banksmen was going to shout the terrible tidings down the shaft; and if Stephen should be near, instead of being at work farther in the pit, the words would fall upon him without any softening or preparation. He implored them to wait until he could run and tell Miss Anne; but while he was speaking they saw Miss Anne herself coming towards the pit, her face very pale and sorrowful, for the rumour had reached the master's house, and she was hastening to meet Stephen, and comfort him, if that were possible.

'Oh, Miss Anne!' cried Tim; 'it will kill poor Stephen, if it come upon him sudden like. I know the way through the old pit to where poor little Nan has fallen; and I'll go and find her. The roof's dropped in, and only a boy could creep along. But who's to tell Stevie? Oh, Miss Anne, couldn't you go down with me, and tell him gently your own self?'

'Yes, I will go,' said Miss Anne, weeping.

Underground, in those low, dark, pent-up galleries, lighted only here and there by a glimmering lamp, the colliers were busy at their labours, unconscious of all that was happening overhead. Stephen was at work at some distance from the others, loading a train of small square waggons with the blocks of coal which he and Black Thompson had picked out of the earth. He was singing softly to himself the hymns that he and little Nan had been learning during the summer in the Red Gravel Pit; and he smiled as he fancied that little Nan was perhaps singing them over as well by the cabin fire. He did not know, poor boy, that at that moment Tim was creeping through the winding, blocked-up passages, so long untrodden, to the bottom of the old shaft; and that when he returned he would be bearing in his arms a sad, sad burden, upon which his tears would fall unavailingly.

Stephen's comrades were all of a sudden very quiet, and their pickaxes no longer gave dull muffled thumps upon the seam of coal; but he was too busy to notice how idle and still they were. It was only when Cole spoke to him, in a tone of extraordinary mildness, that the boy paused in his rough and toilsome employment.

'My lad,' said Cole, 'Miss Anne's come down the pit, and she's asking for thee.'

'She promised she'd come some day,' cried Stephen, with a thrill of pleasure and a quicker throbbing of his heart, as he darted along the narrow paths to the loftier and more open space near the bottom of the shaft, where Miss Anne was waiting for him. The covered lamps gave too little light for him to see how pale and sorrow-stricken she looked; but the solemn tenderness of her voice sank deeply into his heart.

'Stephen, my dear boy,' she said, 'are you sure that I care for you, and would not let any trouble come upon you if I could help it?'

'Yes, surely, Miss Anne,' answered the boy wonderingly.

'Your Father which is in heaven cares much more for you,' she continued; 'but "whom the Lord loveth He chasteneth, and scourgeth every son whom He receiveth." God is dealing with you as His son, Stephen. Can you bear the sorrow which is sent by Him?'

'If the Lord Jesus will help me,' he murmured.

'He will help you, my poor boy,' said Miss Anne 'Oh, Stephen, Stephen, how can I tell you? Our little Nan, our precious little child, has fallen down the old shaft.'

Stephen reeled giddily, and would have sunk to the ground, but Cole held him up in his strong arms, while his comrades gathered about him with tears and sobs, which prevented them uttering any words of consolation. But he could not have listened to them. He fancied he heard the pattering of Nan's little feet, and saw her laughing face. But no! he heard instead the dull and lingering footsteps of Tim, and saw a little lifeless form folded from sight in Tim's jacket.

'The little lass 'ud die very easy,' whispered Cole, passing his arm tighter round Stephen; 'and she's up in heaven among the angels by this time, I reckon.'

Stephen drew himself away from Cole's arm, and staggered forward a step or two to meet Tim; when he took the sad burden from him, and sat down without a word, pressing it closely to his breast. His perfect silence touched all about him. Miss Anne hid her face in her hands, and some of the men groaned aloud.

'The old pit ought to have been bricked up years ago,' said Cole; 'the child's death will be upon the master's head.'

'It'll all go to one reckoning,' muttered Black Thompson. But Stephen seemed not to hear their words. Still, with the child clasped tightly to him, he waited for the lowering of the skip, and when it descended, he seated himself in it without lifting up his head, which was bent over the dead child. Miss Anne and Tim took their places beside him, and they were drawn up to the broad, glittering light of day on the surface, where a crowd of eager bystanders was waiting for Stephen's appearance.

'Don't speak to me, please,' he murmured, without looking round; and they made way for him in his deep, silent grief, as he passed on homewards, followed by Miss Anne. Once she saw him look up to the hills, where, at Fern's Hollow, the new house stood out conspicuously against the snow; and when they passed the shaft, he shuddered visibly; but yet he was silent, and scarcely seemed to know that she was walking beside him.

The cabin was full of women from Botfield, for Martha had fallen into violent fits of hysterics, and none of their remedies had any effect in soothing her. One of them took the dead child from Stephen's arms at the door, and bade him go away and sit in her cottage till she came to him. But he turned off towards the hills; and Miss Anne, seeing that she could say nothing to comfort him just then, watched him strolling along the old road that led to Fern's Hollow, with his arms folded and his head bent down, as if he were still carrying that sad burden which he had borne up from the pit, so closely pressed against his heart.


CHAPTER XV

RENEWED CONFLICT

'I'm a murderer, Miss Anne,' said Martha, with a look of settled despair upon her face, on the evening of the next day.

She had been sitting all the weary hours since morning with her face buried in her hands, hearing and heeding no one, until Miss Anne came and sat down beside her, speaking to her in her own kind and gentle tones. Upon a table in the corner of the cabin lay the little form of the dead child, covered with a white cloth. The old grandfather was crouching over the fire, moaning and laughing by turns; and Stephen was again absent, rambling upon the snowy uplands.

'And for murderers there is pardon,' said Miss Anne softly.

'Oh, I never thought I wanted pardon,' cried Martha; 'I always felt I'd done my duty better than any of the girls about here. But I've killed little Nan; and now I remember how cross I used to be when nobody was nigh, till she grew quite timmer-some of me. Everybody knows I've murdered her; and now it doesn't signify how bad I am. I shall never get over that.'

'Martha,' said Miss Anne, 'you are not so guilty of the child's death as my uncle, who ought to have had the pit bricked over safely when it was no longer in use. But you say you never thought you wanted pardon. Surely you feel your need of it now.'

'But God will never forgive me now,' replied Martha hopelessly; 'I see how wicked I have been, but the chance is gone by. God will not forgive me now; nor Stephen.'

'We will not talk about Stephen,' said Miss Anne; 'but I will tell you about God. When He gave His commandments to mankind that they might obey them, He proclaimed His own name at the same time. Listen to His name, Martha: "The Lord, the Lord God, merciful and gracious, long-suffering, and abundant in goodness and truth, keeping mercy for thousands, forgiving iniquity, transgression, and sin." If you would not go to Him for mercy when you did not feel your need of it, He was keeping it for you against this time; saving and treasuring it up for you, "that He might show the exceeding riches of His grace in His kindness towards us, through Christ Jesus." He is waiting to pardon your iniquity, for Christ's sake. Do you wish to be forgiven now? Do you feel that you are a sinful girl, Martha?'

'I have thought of nothing else all day long,' whispered Martha; 'I have helped to kill little Nan by my sins.'

'Yes,' said Miss Anne mournfully; 'if, like Stephen, you had opened your heart to the gentle teaching of the Holy Spirit, if you had looked to Jesus, trusted in Him, and followed Him, this grief would not have come upon you and upon all of us. For Bess would not have persuaded you to leave your own duties, and little Nan would have been alive still.'

'Oh, I knew I'd killed her!' cried a voice behind them; and, looking round, Miss Anne saw that the door had been softly opened, and Bess had crept in unheard. Her face was swollen with weeping, and she stood wringing her hands, as she cast a fearful glance at the white-covered table in the corner.

'Come here, Bess,' said Miss Anne; and the girl crept to them, and sat down on the ground at their feet. Miss Anne talked long with them about little Nan's death, until they shed many tears in true contrition of heart for their sinfulness; and when they appeared to feel their own utter helplessness, she explained to them, in such simple and easy language as Bess could understand, how they could obtain salvation through faith in the Lord Jesus Christ. After which they all knelt down; and Miss Anne prayed earnestly for the weeping and heart-broken girls, who, as yet, hardly knew how they could frame any prayers for themselves.

When Miss Anne left the cabin the night was quite dark but the snow which lay unmelted on the mountains showed their outlines plainly with a pale gleaming of light though the sky was overcast with more snow-clouds. Her heart was full of sadness for Stephen, who was wandering, no one knew whither, among the snowdrifts on the solitary plains. She knew that he must be passing through a terrible trial and temptation, but she could do nothing for him; her voice could not reach him, nor her eye tell him by a silent look how deeply she felt for him. Yet Miss Anne knew who it is that possesseth 'the shields of the earth,' and in her earnest thanksgiving to God for Martha and Bess Thompson, she prayed fervently that the boy might be shielded and sheltered in his great sorrow, and that when he was tried he might come forth as gold.

All the day long, Stephen, instead of going to his work in the pit, had been rambling, without aim or purpose, over the dreary uplands; here and there stretching himself upon the wiry heath, where the sun had dried away the snow, and hiding his face from the light, while he gave way to an anguish of grief, and broke the deep silence with a loud and very bitter cry. It was death, sudden death, he was lamenting. Only yesterday morning little Nan was clinging strongly to his neck, and covering his face with merry kisses; and every now and then he felt as if he was only dreaming, and he started down towards home, as though he could not believe that those tender arms were stiffened and that rosy mouth still in death. But before he could run many paces the truth was borne in upon his aching heart that she was surely dead; and never more in this life would he see and speak to her, or listen to her lisping tongue. Little Nan, dearest of all earthly things,—perhaps dearer to him in the infancy of his Christian life than the Saviour Himself,—was removed from him so far that she was already a stranger, and he knew nothing of her.

Towards evening he found himself, in his aimless wandering, drawing near to Fern's Hollow, where she had lived. The outer shell of the new house was built up, the three rooms above and below, with the little dairy and coal-shed beside them, and Stephen, even in his misery, was glad of the shelter of the blank walls from the cutting blast of the north wind; for he felt that he could not go home to the cabin where the dead child—no longer darling little Nan—was lying. Poor Stephen! He sat down on a heap of bricks upon the new hearth, where no household fire had ever been kindled; and, while the snow-flakes drifted in upon him unheeded, he buried his face again in his hands, and went on thinking, as he had been doing all day. He would never care to come back now to Fern's Hollow. No! he would get away to some far-off country, where he should never more hear the master's name spoken. Let him keep the place, he thought, and let it be a curse to him, for he had bought it with a child's blood. If the law gave him back Fern's Hollow, it would not avenge little Nan's death; and he had no power. But the master was a murderer; and Stephen knelt down on the desolate hearth, where no prayer had ever been uttered, and prayed God that the sin and punishment of murder might rest upon his enemy.

Was it consolation that filled Stephen's heart when he rose from his knees? It seemed as if his spirit had grown suddenly harder, and in some measure stronger. He did not feel afraid now of going down to the cabin, where the little lifeless corpse was stretched out; and he strode away down the hill with rapid steps. When the thought of Martha, and his grandfather, and Miss Anne crossed his mind, it was with no gentle, tender emotion, but with a strange feeling that he no longer cared for them. All his love was gone with little Nan. Only the thought of the master, and the terrible reckoning that lay before him, sent a thrill through his heart. 'I shall be there at the judgment,' he muttered half aloud, looking up to the cold, cloudy sky, almost as if he expected to see the sign of the coming of the Lord. But there was no sign there; and, after gazing for a minute or two, he turned in the direction of the cabin, where he could see a glimmer of the light within through the chinks of the door and shutter.

Bess and Martha were still sitting hand in hand as Miss Anne had left them; but they both started up as Stephen entered, pale and ghastly from his long conflict with grief and temptation on the hills. He was come home conquered, though he did not know it; and the expression of his face was one of hatred and vengeance, instead of sorrow and love. He bade Black Bess to be off out of his sight in a voice so changed and harsh, that both the girls were frightened, and Martha stole away tremblingly with her. He was alone then, with his sleeping grandfather on the bed, and the dead child lying in the corner, from which he carefully averted his eyes; when there came a quiet tap at the door, and, before he could answer, it was slowly opened, and the master stepped into the cabin. He stood before the boy, looking into his white face in silence, and when he spoke his voice was very husky and low.

'My lad,' he said, 'I'm very sorry for you; and I'll have the pit bricked over at once. It had slipped my memory, Stephen; but Martha knew of it, and she ought to have taken better care of the child. It is no fault of mine; or it is only partly my fault, at any rate. But, whether or no, I'm come to tell you I'm willing to bear the expenses of the funeral in reason; and here's a sovereign for you besides, my lad.'

The master held out a glittering sovereign in his hand, but Stephen pushed it away, and, seizing his arm firmly, drew him, reluctant as he was, to the white-covered table in the corner. There was no look of pain upon the pale, placid little features before them; but there was an awful stillness, and all the light of life was gone out of the open eyes, which were fixed into an upward gaze. The Bible, which Stephen had not looked for that morning, had been used instead of a cushion, and the motionless head lay upon it.

'That was little Nan yesterday,' said Stephen hoarsely; 'she is gone to tell God all about you. You robbed us of our own home; and you've been the death of little Nan. God's curse will be upon you. It's no use my cursing; I can do nothing; but God can punish you better than me. A while ago I thought I'd get away to some other country where I'd never hear of you; but I'll wait now, if I'm almost clemmed to death, till

I see what God will do at you. Take your money. You've robbed me of all I love, but I won't take from you what you love. I'll only wait here till I see what God can do.'

He loosed his grasp then, and opened the door wide. The master muttered a few words indistinctly, but he did not linger in the cabin beside that awful little corpse. The night had already deepened into intense darkness; and Stephen, standing at the door to listen, thought, with a quick tingling through all his veins, that perhaps the master would himself fall down the open pit. But no, he passed on securely; and Martha, coming in shortly afterwards, ventured to remark that she had just brushed against the master in the lane, and wondered where he was going to at that time of night.

Miss Anne came to see Stephen the next day; but, though he seemed to listen to her respectfully, she felt that she had lost her influence over him; and she could do nothing for him but intercede with God that the Holy Spirit, who only can enter into our inmost souls and waken there every memory, would in His own good time recall to Stephen's heart all the lessons of love and forgiveness he had been learning, and enable him to overcome the evil spirit that had gained the mastery over him.

All the people in Botfield wished to attend little Nan's funeral, but Stephen would not consent to it. At first he said only Tim and himself should accompany the tiny coffin to the churchyard at Longville; but Martha implored so earnestly to go with them, that he was compelled to relent. The coffin was placed in a little cart, drawn by one of the hill-ponies, and led slowly by Tim; while Stephen and Martha walked behind, the latter weeping many humble and repentant tears, as she thought sorrowfully of little Nan; but Stephen with a set and gloomy face, and a heart that pondered only upon the calamities that should overtake his enemy.


CHAPTER XVI

SOFTENING THOUGHTS

But God had not forsaken Stephen; though, for a little time, He had left him to the working of his own sinful nature, that he might know of a certainty that in himself there dwelt no good thing. God looks down from heaven upon all our bitter conflicts; and He weighs, as a just Judge, all the events that happen on earth. From the servant to whom He has given but one talent, He does not demand the same service as from him who has ten talents. Stephen's heavenly Father knew exactly how much understanding and strength he possessed, for He Himself had given those good gifts to the boy, and He knew in what measure He had bestowed them. When the right time was come, 'He sent from above, He took him, He brought him out of many waters. He brought him forth also into a large place; He delivered him, because He delighted in him.'

After the great tribulation of those days Stephen fell into a long and severe illness. For many weeks he was delirious and unconscious, neither knowing what he said nor who was taking care of him. When Miss Anne sat beside him, soothing him, as she sometimes could do, with singing, he would talk of being in heaven, and listening to little Nan among the angels. Bess shared many of Martha's weary hours of watching: and so deeply had the child's death affected them, that now all their thoughts and talk were about the things that Miss Anne diligently taught them concerning Jesus and His salvation. It was not much they knew; but as in former times a very small subject was sufficient for a long gossip, so now the little knowledge of the Scriptures that was lodged in either of their minds became the theme of fluent, if not very learned conversation. Sometimes Stephen, as if their words caught some floating memory, would murmur out a verse or two in his delirious ramblings, or sing part of a hymn. Tim, also, who came for an hour or two every evening, was always ready to read the few chapters he had learned, and to give the girls his interpretation of them.

There was no pressing want in the little household, though their bread-winner was unable to work. The miners made up Stephen's wages among themselves at every reckoning, for Stephen had won their sincere respect, though they had often been tempted to ill-treat him. Miss Anne came every day with dainties from the master's house, without meeting with any reproof or opposition, though the name of Stephen Fern never crossed Mr. Wyley's lips. Still he used to listen attentively whenever the doctor called upon Miss Anne, to give her his opinion how the poor boy was going on.

When Stephen was recovering, his mind was too weak for any of the violent passions that had preceded his illness. Moreover, the bounty of his comrades, and the humble kindness of Martha and Bess, came like healing to his soul; for very often the tenderness of others will seem to atone for the injuries of our enemies, and at least soften our vehement desire for revenge. Yet, in a quiet, listless sort of way, Stephen still longed for God to prove His wrath against the master's wrong-doing. It appeared so strange to hear that all this time nothing had befallen him, that he was still strong and healthy, and becoming more and more wealthy every day. Like Asaph, the psalmist, when he considered the prosperity of the wicked, Stephen was inclined to say, 'How doth God know? and is there knowledge with the Most High? Behold, these are the ungodly that prosper in the earth; they increase in riches. Verily I have cleansed my heart in vain, and washed my hands in innocency. For all the day long have I been plagued, and chastened every morning.'

'Why does God let these things be?' he inquired of Miss Anne one day, after he was well enough to rise from his bed and sit by the fire. He was very white and thin, and his eyes looked large and shining in their sunken sockets; but they gazed earnestly into his teacher's face, as if he was craving to have this difficulty solved.

'You have asked me a hard question,' said Miss Anne; 'we cannot understand God's way, for "as the heavens are higher than the earth, so are His ways than our ways." But shall we try to find out a reason why God let these things be for little Nan's sake?'

'Yes,' said Stephen, turning away his eyes from her face.

'Our Lord Jesus Christ had one disciple, called John, whom He loved more than the rest; and before John died he was permitted to see heaven, and to write down many of the things shown to him, that we also might know of them. He beheld a holy city, whose builder and maker is God, and having the glory of God. It was built, as it were, of pure gold, and the walls were of all manner of precious stones; the gates of the city were of pearl, and the streets of gold, as clear and transparent as glass. There was no need of the sun nor of the moon to shine in it; for the glory of God doth lighten it, and the Lamb is the light thereof. He saw, too, the throne of God, and above it there was a rainbow of emerald, which was a sign of His covenant with the people upon earth. And round about the throne, nearer than the angels, there were seats, upon which men who had been ransomed from this world of sin and sorrow were sitting in white robes, and with crowns upon their heads. There came a pure river of water of life out of the throne, and on each side of the river, in the streets of the city, there was a tree of life, the leaves of which are for the healing of all nations. Before the throne stood a great multitude, which no man could number, clothed in white robes, and with palms in their hands. And as John listened, he heard a sound like the voice of many waters; then, as it became clearer, it seemed like the voice of a great thunder; but at last it rang down into his opened ears as the voice of many harpers, singing a new song with their harps. And he heard a great voice out of heaven, proclaiming the covenant of God with men: "Behold, the tabernacle of God is with men, and He will dwell with them, and they shall be His people; and God Himself shall be with them, and be their God. And God shall wipe away all tears from their eyes; and there shall be no more death, neither sorrow, nor crying, neither shall there be any more pain." The disciple whom Jesus loved saw many other things which he was commanded to seal up; but these things were written for our comfort.'

'And little Nan is there,' murmured Stephen, as the tears rolled down his cheeks.

'Our Lord says of little children, "I say unto you, that in heaven their angels do always behold the face of my Father which is in heaven,"' continued Miss Anne. 'Stephen, do you wish her to be back again in this sorrowful world, with Martha and you for companions, instead of the angels?'

'Oh no!' sobbed Stephen.

'And now, why has God sent so many troubles to you, my poor Stephen? As I told you before, we cannot understand His ways yet. But do not you see that sorrow has made you very different to the other boys about you? Have you not gained much wisdom that they do not possess? And would you change your lot with any one of them? Would you even be as you were yourself twelve months ago, before these afflictions came? We are sent into this world for something more than food and clothing, and work and play. Our souls must live, and they are dead if they are not brought into submission to God's will. Even our own Lord and Saviour, "though He were a son, yet learned He obedience by the things which He suffered." How much more do we need to suffer before we learn obedience to the will of God!

'Then there is Martha,' continued Miss Anne, after a pause; 'she and Bess are both brought to repentance by the death of our little child. Surely I need not excuse God's dealings to you any more, Stephen.'

'But there comes no judgment upon the master,' said Stephen in a low voice.

A flush of pain passed over Miss Anne's face as she met Stephen's eager gaze, and saw something of the working of his heart in his flashing eye.

'Our God will suffer no sin to go unpunished for ever,' she answered solemnly. '"Vengeance is mine; I will repay, saith the Lord." Listen, Stephen: when our Lord spoke those "blessings" in your chapter, He implied that on the opposite side there were curses corresponding to them. But He did not leave this matter uncertain; I will read them to you from another chapter: "But woe unto you that are rich! for ye have received your consolation. Woe unto you that are full! for ye shall hunger. Woe unto you that laugh now! for ye shall mourn and lament."'

'That is the master,' said Stephen, his face glowing with satisfaction, 'for he is rich and full, and he laughs now!'

'Yes, who can tell but that these woes will fall upon my uncle,' said Miss Anne, and her head drooped low, and Stephen saw the tears streaming down her cheeks; 'all my prayers and love for him may be lost. His soul, which is as precious and immortal as ours, may perish for ever!'

Stephen looked at her bitter weeping with a longing desire to say something to comfort her, but he could not speak a word: for her grief was caused by the thought of the very vengeance he was wishing for. He turned away his head uneasily, and gazed deep down into the glowing embers of the fire.

'Not my prayers and love only,' continued Miss Anne, 'but our Saviour's also; all His griefs and sorrows may prove unavailing, as far as my uncle is concerned. Perhaps He will say of him, "I have laboured in vain, I have spent My strength for nought, and in vain." O my Saviour! because I love Thee, I would have every immortal soul saved for Thy eternal glory.'

'And so would I, Miss Anne,' cried the boy, sinking on his knees. 'Oh, Miss Anne, pray to Jesus that I may love all my enemies for His sake.'

When Miss Anne's prayer was ended, she left Stephen alone to the deep but gentler thoughts that were filling his mind. He understood now, with a clearness that he had never had before, that 'love is of God; and every one that loveth is born of God, and knoweth God.' He must love his enemies because they were precious, as he himself had been, in all their sin and rebellion, to their Father in heaven. Not only did God send rain and sunshine upon the evil and unjust, but He had so loved them as to give His only begotten Son to die for them; and if they perished, so far it made the cross of Christ of none effect. Henceforth the bitterness of revenge died out of his heart; and whenever he bent his knees in prayer, he offered up the dying petition of his namesake, the martyr Stephen, in behalf of all his enemies, but especially of his master: 'Lord, lay not this sin to their charge.'


CHAPTER XVII

A NEW CALLING

Stephen's recovery went on so slowly, that the doctor who attended him said it would not be fit for him to resume his underground labour for some months to come, if he were ever able to do so; and advised him to seek some out-door employment. His old comrades began to find the weekly subscription to make up his wages rather a tax upon their own earnings; and Stephen himself was unwilling to be a burden upon them any longer. As soon, therefore, as he was strong enough to bear the journey, he resolved to cross the hills again to Danesford, to see when Mr. Lockwood was coming home, and what help the clergyman left in charge of his duty could give to him. Tim brought his father's donkey for him to ride, and went with him across the uplands. The hard frosts and the snow were over, for it was past the middle of March; but the house at Fern's Hollow remained in precisely the same state as when little Nan died; not a stroke of work had been done at it, and a profound silence brooded over the place. Perhaps the master had lost all pleasure in his ill-gotten possession!

So changed was Stephen, though Danesford looked exactly the same, so tall had he grown during his illness, and so white was his formerly brown face, that the big boy who had shown him the way to the rectory did not know him again in the least. Probably Mr. Lockwood and his daughter would not have recognised him; but they were still lingering in a warmer climate, until the east winds had quite finished their course. The strange clergyman, however, was exceedingly kind to both the boys, and promised to send a full and faithful account to Mr. Lockwood of all the circumstances they narrated to him; for Tim told of many things which Stephen passed over. They had done right in coming to him, he said; and he gave Stephen enough money to supply the immediate necessities of his family, at the same time bidding him apply for more if he needed any; for he knew that a boy of his principle and character would never live upon other people's charity whenever he could work for himself.

How refreshing and strengthening it was upon the tableland that spring afternoon! The red leaf-buds of the bilberry-wires were just bursting forth, and the clumps of gorse were tinged with the first golden flowers. Every kind of moss was there carpeting the ground with a bright fresh green from the moisture of the spring showers. As for the birds, they seemed absolutely in a frenzy of enjoyment, and seemed to forget that they had their nests to build as they flew from bush to bush, singing merrily in the sunshine.

Tim wrapped a cloak round Stephen; and then they faced the breeze gaily, as it swept to meet them with a pure breath over miles of heath and budding flowers. No wonder that Stephen's heart rose within him with a rekindled gladness and gratitude; while Tim became almost as wild as the birds. But Stephen began to feel a little tired as they neared Fern's Hollow, though they were still two miles from the cinder-hill cabin.

'Home, home!' he said, rather mournfully, pointing to the new house. 'Tim, I remember I used to feel in myself as if that was to be my own home for ever. I didn't think that God only meant it to be mine for a little while, even if I kept it till I died. And when I thought I was going to die, it seemed as if it didn't signify what kind of a place we'd lived in, or what troubles had happened to us. Yesterday, Tim, Miss Anne showed me a verse about us being strangers and pilgrims upon the earth.'

'Perhaps we are pilgrims,' replied Tim, 'but we aren't much strangers on these hills.'

'It means,' said Stephen, 'that we are no more at home here than a stranger is when he is passing through Botfield. I'm willing now never to go back to Fern's Hollow, if God pleases. Not that little Nan is gone; but because I'm sure God will do what is best with me, and we're to have no continuing city here. I think I shouldn't feel a bit angry if I saw other people living there.'

'Hillo! what's that?' cried Tim.

Surely it could not be smoke from the top of the new chimney? Yes; a thin, clear blue column of smoke was curling briskly up into the air, and then floating off in a banner over the hillside. Somebody was there, that was certain; and the first fire had been lighted on the hearthstone. There was a sharp pang in Stephen's heart, and he cast down his eyes for a moment, but then he looked up to the sky above him with a smile; while Tim set up a loud shout, and urged the donkey to a canter.

'It's Martha!' he cried; 'I saw her gown peeping round the corner of the wall. I'll lay a wager it's her print gown. Come thy ways; we'll make sure afore we pass.'

It was Martha waiting for them at the old wicket, and Bess was just within the doorway. They were come so far to meet the travellers, and had even prepared tea for them in the new kitchen, having cleared away some of the bricks and mortar, and raised benches with the pieces of planks left about. Tea was just ready for Stephen's refreshment, and he felt that he was in the greatest need of it; so they sat down to it as soon as Martha had laid out the provisions, among which was a cake sent by Miss Anne. The fire of wood-chips blazed brightly, and gave out a pleasant heat; and every one of the little party felt a quiet enjoyment, though there were many tender thoughts of little Nan.

'We may be pilgrims,' said Tim reflectively, over a slice of cake, 'but there's lots of pleasant things sent us by the way.'

They were still at tea when the gamekeeper, who was passing by, and who guessed from the smoke from the chimney, and the donkey grazing in the new pasture, that some gipsies had taken possession of Fern's Hollow, came to look through the unglazed window. He had not seen Stephen since his illness, and there was something in his wasted face and figure which touched even him.

'I'm sorry to see thee looking so badly, my lad,' he said; 'I must speak to my missis to send you something nourishing, for I've not forgotten you, Stephen. If ever there comes a time when I can speak up about any business of yours without hurting myself, you may depend upon me; but I don't like making enemies, and the Bible says we must live peaceably with all men. I heard talk of you wanting some out-door work for a while; and there's my wife's brother is wanting a shepherd's boy. He'd take you at my recommendation, and I'd be glad to speak a word for you. Would that do for you?'

Stephen accepted the offer gladly; and when the gamekeeper was gone, they sang a hymn together, so blotting out by an offering of praise the evil prayer which he had uttered upon that hearth on the night of his desolation and strong conflict. Pleasant was the way home to the old cabin in the twilight; pleasant the hearty 'Good-night' of Tim and Bess; but most pleasant of all was the calm sense of truth, and the submissive will with which Stephen resigned himself to the providence of God.

The work of a shepherd was far more to Stephen's taste than his dangerous toil as a collier. From his earliest years he had been accustomed to wander with his grandfather over the extensive sheep-walks, seeking out any strayed lambs, or diligently gathering food for the sick ones of the flock. To be sure, he could only earn little more than half his former wages, and his time for returning from his work would always be uncertain, and often very late. But then, sorrowful consideration! there was no little Nan to provide for now, nor to fill up his leisure hours at home. Martha was earning money for herself; and as yet the master had demanded no rent for their miserable cabin; so his earnings as a shepherd's boy would do until Mr. Lockwood came back. Still upon the mountains he would be exposed to the bleak winds and heavy storms of the spring; while underground the temperature had always been the same. No wonder that Miss Anne, when she looked at the boy's wasted and enfeebled frame, listened with unconcealed anxiety to his new project for gaining his livelihood; and so often as the spring showers swept in swift torrents across the sky, lifted up her eyes wistfully to the unsheltered mountains, as she pictured Stephen at the mercy of the pitiless storm.

CHAPTER XVIII

THE PANTRY WINDOW

Stephen had been engaged in his new calling for about a fortnight, and was coming home, after a long and toilsome day among the flocks, two hours after sunset, with a keen east wind bringing the tears into his eyes, when a few paces from his cabin door a tall dark figure sprang up from a hollow in the cinder-hill, and laid a heavy hand upon his shoulder. It was just light enough to discern the gloomy features of Black Thompson; and Stephen inquired fearlessly what he wanted with him.

'I thought thee'd never be coming,' said Black Thompson impatiently. 'Lad, hast thee forgotten thy rights and thy wrongs, that thou comes to yonder wretched kennel whistling as if all the land belonged to thee? Where's thy promise to thy father, that thee'd never give up thy rights? Jackson the butcher has taken Fern's Hollow, and it's to be finished up in a week or two; and thee'lt see thy own place go into the hands of strangers.'

'It'll all be put right some day, Thompson, thank you,' said Stephen.

'Right!' repeated Thompson; 'who's to put wrong things right if we won't take the trouble ourselves? Is it right for the master to grind us down in our wages, and raise the rents over our heads, till we can scarcely get enough to keep us in victuals, just that he may add money to money to count over of nights? Was it right of him to leave the pit yonder open, till little Nan was killed in it? Thee has a heavy reckoning to settle with him, and I'd be wiping off some of the score. If I was in thy place, I should have little Nan's voice calling me day and night from the pit, to ask when I was going to revenge her.'

Black Thompson felt that Stephen trembled under his grasp, and he went on with greater earnestness.

'Thee could revenge thyself this very night. Thee could get the worth of Fern's Hollow without a risk, if thee'd listen to me. It's thy own, lad, and thy wrongs are heavy—Fern's Hollow stolen from thee, and the little lass murdered! How canst thee rest, Stephen?'

'God will repay,' said Stephen in a tremulous tone.

'Dost think that God sees?' asked Black Thompson scoffingly; 'if He sees, He doesn't care. What does it matter to Him that poor folks like us are trodden down and robbed? If He cared, He could strike the master dead in a moment, and He doesn't. He lets him prosper and prosper, till nobody can stand afore him. I'd take my own matter in my own hands, and make sure of vengeance. God doesn't take any notice.'

'I'm sure God sees,' answered Stephen; 'He is everywhere; and He isn't blind, or deaf, only we don't understand what He is going to do yet. If He didn't take any notice of us, He wouldn't make me feel so happy, spite of everything. Oh, Thompson thee and the men were so kind to me when I couldn't work, and I've never seen thee to thank thee. I can do nothing for thee, except I could persuade thee to repent, and be as happy as I am.'

'Oh, I'll repent some day,' said Black Thompson, loosing Stephen's arm; 'but I've lots of things to do aforehand, and I reckon they can all be repented of together. So, lad, it's true what everybody is saying of thee—thee has forgotten poor little Nan, and thy promise to thy father!'

'No, I've never forgotten,' replied Stephen, 'but I'll never try to revenge myself now. I couldn't if I did try. Besides, I've forgiven the master; so don't speak to me again about it, Thompson.'

'Well, lad, be sure I'll never waste my time thinking of thee again,' said Black Thompson, with an oath; 'thy religion has made a poor, spiritless, cowardly chap of thee, and I've done with thee altogether.'

Black Thompson strode away into the darkness, and was quickly out of hearing, while Stephen stood still and listened to his rapid footsteps, turning over in his mind what mischief he wished to tempt him to now. The open shaft was only a few feet from him; but it had been safely encircled by a high iron railing, instead of being bricked over, as it had been found of use in the proper ventilation of the pit. From Thompson and his temptation, Stephen's thoughts went swiftly to little Nan, and how he had heard her calling to him upon that dreadful night when he went away with the poachers. Was it possible that he could forget her for a single day? Was she not still one of his most constant and most painful thoughts? Yes, he could remember every pretty look of her face, and every sweet sound of her voice; yet they were saying he had forgotten her, while the pit was there for him to pass night and morning—a sorrowful reminder of her dreadful death! A sharp thrill ran through Stephen's frame as his outstretched hand caught one of the iron railings, which rattled in its socket; but his very heart stood still when up from the dark, narrow depths there came a low and stifled cry of 'Stephen! Stephen!'

He was no coward, though Black Thompson had called him one; but this voice from the dreaded pit, at that dark and lonely hour, made him tremble so greatly that he could neither move nor shout aloud for very fear. He leaned there, holding fast by the railing, with his hearing made wonderfully acute, and his eyes staring blindly into the dense blackness beneath him. In another second he detected a faint glimmer, like a glow-worm deep down in the earth, and the voice, still muffled and low, came up to him again.

'It's only me—Tim!' it cried. 'Hush! don't speak, Stephen; don't make any noise. I'm left down in the pit. They're going to break into the master's house to-night. They're going to get thee to creep through the pantry window. If thee won't, Jack Davies is to go. They'll fire the thatch, if they can't get the door open. Thee go and take care of Miss Anne, and send Martha to Longville for help. Don't trust anybody at Botfield.'

These sentences sounded up into Stephen's ears, one by one, slowly, as Tim could give his voice its due tone and strength. He recollected instantly all the long oppression the men had suffered from their master. In that distant part of the county, where there were extensive works, the colliers had been striking for larger wages; and some of them had strolled down to Botfield, bringing with them an increase of discontent and inquietude, which had taken deep root in the minds of all the workpeople. It was well known that the master kept large sums of money in his house, which, as I have told you, was situated among lonely fields, nearly a mile from Botfield; and no one lived with him, except Miss Anne, and one maid-servant. It was a very secure building, with stone casements and strongly barred doors; but if a boy could get through the pantry window, he could admit the others readily. How long it would be before the attempt was made Stephen could not tell, but it was already late, and Black Thompson had left him hurriedly. But at least it must be an hour or two nearer midnight, and all hopes of rescue and defence rested upon him and Martha only.

Martha was sitting by the fire knitting, and Bess Thompson was pinning on her shawl to go home. Poor Bess! Even in his excitement Stephen felt for her; but he dared not utter a word till she was gone. But then Martha could not credit his hurried tidings and directions, until she had been herself to the shaft to see the feeble gleam of Tim's lamp, and hear the sound of his voice; for as soon as she rattled the railings he spoke again.

'Be sharp!' he cried. 'I'm not afeared; but I can't stay here where little Nan died. I'll go back to the pit, and wait till morning. Be sharp!'

There was no need after that to urge Martha to hasten. After throwing a shawl over her head, she started off for Longville with the swiftness of a hare; and was soon past the engine-house, and threading her way cautiously through Botfield, where she dreaded to be discovered as she passed the lighted windows, or across the gleam of some open door. Many of the houses were quite closed up and dark, but in some there was a voice of talking; and here and there Martha saw a figure stealing like herself along the deepest shadows. But she escaped without being noticed; and, once through the village, her path lay along the silent high-roads straight on to Longville.

Nor did Stephen linger in the cinder-hill cabin. He ran swiftly over the pit-banks, and stole along by the limekilns and the blacksmith's shop, for under the heavy door he could see a little fringe of light. How loudly the dry cinders cranched under his careful footsteps! Yet, quiet as the blacksmith's shop was, and soundless as the night without, the noise did not reach the ears of those who were lurking within, and Stephen went on in safety. There stood the master's house at last, black and massive-looking against the dark sky; not a gleam from fire or candle to be seen below, for every window was closely shuttered; but on the second storey there shone a lighted casement, which Stephen knew belonged to the master's chamber. The dog, which came often with Miss Anne to the cinder-hill cabin, gave one loud bay, and then sprang playfully upon Stephen, as if to apologize for his mistake in barking at him. For some minutes the boy stood in deep deliberation, scarcely daring to knock at the door, lest some of the housebreakers should be already concealed near the spot, and rush upon him before it was opened, or else enter with him into the defenceless dwelling. But at length he gave one very quiet rap with his fingers, and after a minute's pause his heart bounded with joy as he heard Miss Anne herself asking who was there.

'Stephen Fern,' he answered, with his lips close to the keyhole, and speaking in his lowest tones.

'What is the matter, Stephen?' she asked. 'I cannot open the door, for my uncle always takes the keys with him into his own room.'

'Please to take the light into the pantry for one minute,' he whispered cautiously, with a fervent hope that Miss Anne would do so without requiring any further explanations; for he was lost if Black Thompson or Davies were lying in wait near at hand. Very thankfully he heard Miss Anne's step across the quarried floor, and in a moment afterwards the light shone through a low window close by. It was unglazed, with a screen of open lattice-work over it so as to allow of free ventilation. It had one thick stone upright in the middle, leaving such a narrow space as only a boy could creep through. He examined the opening quickly and carefully while the light remained, and when Miss Anne returned to the door he whispered again through the keyhole, 'Don't be afraid. It's me—Stephen; I'm coming in through the pantry window.'

He knew his danger. He knew if any of the robbers came up they must hear him removing the wooden lattice which was laid over the opening; and unless they supposed it to be one of their accomplices at work, he would be at once in their power, exposed to their ill-treatment, or perhaps suffer death at their hands. And would Miss Anne within trust to him instead of alarming the master? If he came down and opened the door, all the designs of the evil men would be hastened and finished before Martha could return from Longville. But Stephen did not listen, nor did his fingers tremble over their work, though there was a rush of thoughts and fears through his brain. He tore away the lattice as quickly and quietly as he could, and, with one keen glance round at the dark night, he thrust his head through the narrow frame. He found it was just possible to crush through; and, after a minute's struggle, his feet rested upon the pantry floor.

CHAPTER XIX

FIRE! FIRE!

Anne was standing close to the pantry door, listening to Stephen's mysterious movements in utter bewilderment, hardly knowing whether she ought to call her uncle, but not coming to a decision about it until the boy appeared before her. His first quick action was to secure the door by fastening a rusty bolt which was on the outside, and then, in a few hurried sentences, he explained his strange conduct by telling her how Tim had conveyed to him the design of some of the colliers for breaking into the master's house. There had been several similar robberies in the country during the strike for wages, and Miss Anne was greatly alarmed, while Stephen felt all the tender spirit of a brave man aroused within him, as she sank faint and trembling upon the nearest seat.

'Don't be afraid,' he said courageously; 'they shall tear me to pieces afore they touch you, Miss Anne. I'm stronger than you'd think; but if I can't take care of thee, God can. Hasn't He sent me here, afore they come, on purpose? They'd have come upon you unawares, but for God.'

'You are right, Stephen,' answered Miss Anne. 'He says, "Thou shalt not be afraid for the terror by night." But what shall we do? How can we make ourselves safer? I'll try not to be afraid; but we must do all we can ourselves. Hark! there's a footstep already!'

Yes, there was a footstep, and not a very stealthy one, approaching the house, and the dog bounded forward to the full length of his chain, but he was beaten down with a blow that stunned him. The men were too strong in numbers, and too secure in the extreme loneliness of the dwelling, to care about taking many precautions. Miss Anne and Stephen heard Mr. Wyley cross the floor of his room above, and open his window; but there was silence again, and the chime of the house clock striking eleven was the only sound that broke the silence until the casement above was reclosed, and the master's footfall returned across the room.

'I must go and tell him,' said Miss Anne; 'perhaps he can secure some of his money, lest Martha should be stopped on the way, or not come in time. Stay here and watch, Stephen, and let me know if you hear anything.'

She stole up-stairs in the dark, lest those without should see the glimmer of her candle through the fanlight in the hall; and then she spoke softly to her uncle through his locked and bolted door. Down-stairs Stephen listened with his quickened hearing to the footsteps gathering round the house; and presently the latch of the pantry door was lifted with a sudden click that made him start and catch his breath; but Jack Davies could come no further, now the rusty bolt was drawn on the outside. There was a whispered conversation through the pantry window, and the sound of some one getting out again; and then Stephen crept across the dark kitchen into the hall through which Miss Anne had gone. At the head of the staircase was the door of the master's room, now standing open; and the light from it served to guide him across the strange hall, and up the stairs, until he reached the doorway, and could look in. The chamber had a low and sloping ceiling, and a gable-window in the roof, which was defended by strong bars. Near this window was an open cabinet, containing many little drawers and divisions, all of which were filled with papers; while upon a leaf in the front there lay rolls of bank notes, and heaps of golden money, which the master had been counting over. He stood beside his cabinet as if he had just risen from this occupation, and was leaning upon his chair, panic-stricken at the tidings Miss Anne had uttered. His grey hair was scattered over his forehead, instead of being smoothly brushed back; and the long, loose coat, which hung carelessly around his shrivelled form and stooping shoulders, made him look far older than he did in the day-time. As Stephen's eyes rested upon the sunken form and quaking limbs of the aged man, he felt, for the first time, how helpless and infirm his enemy was, instead of the rich, full, and prospering master he had always considered him.

'Keep off!' cried the old miser, as he caught sight of Stephen on the threshold; and he raised his withered arm as if to ward him from his treasures. 'Keep off! Stephen Fern, is it you? You've come to take your revenge. The robbers and murderers have got in! O God, have pity upon me!'

'I'm come to take care of Miss Anne,' said Stephen, 'They've not got in yet, master. And, please God, help will be here afore long with Martha. The doors and windows are safe.'

'Anne, take him away!' implored Mr. Wyley. 'I don't know if it is true, but take him away. I'm not safe while he's there; they will murder me! Go, go!'

Miss Anne led Stephen away; and no sooner were they outside the room, than the master rushed forward and locked and barred the door securely behind them. There was a window in the landing, looking over the yard where the housebreakers were, and they stood at it in silence, straining their eyes into the darkness. But it did not remain dark long; for a thin, bright flame burst up from behind the dairy wall, and by its fitful blaze they could see the figures of four men coming rapidly round from that corner of the old building.

'Fire! fire!' they shouted, in wild voices of alarm, and beating the iron-studded door with heavy sticks. 'Wake up, master! wake up! the house is on fire!'

Their only answer was a frantic scream from the servant, who thrust her head out of her window, and echoed their shouts with piercing cries. But Stephen and Miss Anne did not move; only Miss Anne laid her hand upon his arm, and he felt how much she trembled.

'They're only trying to frighten us,' he said quietly; 'that's only the wood-stack on fire. They think to frighten us to open the door, by making believe that the house is on fire. Miss Anne, I'm praying to God all the while to send Martha in time.'

'So am I,' she answered, sobbing; 'but oh, Stephen, I am frightened.'

'Miss Anne,' he said, in a comforting tone, 'that chapter about faith you've been teaching me, it says something about quenching fire.'

'"Quenched the violence of fire,"' she murmured; '"out of weakness were made strong."'

She hid her face for a minute or two in both her hands; and then she was strong enough to go to the servant's room, where the terrified girl was still calling for help. The wild shouts and the deafening clamour at the door rang through the house; but the blaze was gone down again; and when Stephen threw open the window just over the heads of the group of men in the yard below, there was not light enough for him to distinguish their faces.

'I'm here,' he said,—'Stephen Fern. I found out what you are up to, and Martha's gone to Longville for help. She'll be here afore long, and you can't force the door open. Put out the fire in the wood-stack, and go home. Maybe if you're not found here you'll get off; for I've seen none of you, and I can only guess at who you are. Go home, I say.'

There was a low, deep growl of disappointment, and a hurried consultation among the men. But whether they would follow Stephen's counsel, it was not permitted them to choose; for suddenly a strong, bright flame burst up in a high column, like a beacon, into the midnight air, and every one gazing upwards saw in a moment that the thatch over the farthest gable had caught fire. The house itself was now burning, and the light, blazing full upon their upturned faces, revealed to Stephen the well-known features of four of his former comrades. The shout that rang from their lips was one of real alarm now.

'Stephen, lad, open the door!' cried Black Thompson. 'We thought to smoke the old fox out of his kennel, but it's took fire in earnest. We'll not hurt him, nor Miss Anne. Lad! the old house will burn like tinder.'

What a glaring light spread through the landing! The face of Miss Anne coming from the servant's room shone rosy and bright in it, though she was pale with fear. Through the open window drifted a suffocating smoke of burning wood and thatch, and the crackling and splitting of the old roof sounded noisily above their voices; but Miss Anne commanded herself, and spoke calmly to Stephen.

'We must open the door to them now,' she said; 'God will protect us from these wicked men. Uncle! uncle! the house is really on fire, and we want the keys. Let me in.'

She knocked loudly at his door, and lifted up her voice to make him hear, and Stephen shouted; but there was no answer. Without the keys of the massive locks it would not be possible to open the doors, and he had them in his own keeping; but he gave no heed to their calls, nor the vehement screams of the frightened servant. Perhaps he had fallen into a fit; and they had no means of entering his chamber, so securely had he fastened himself in with his gold. Stephen and Miss Anne gazed at one another in the dazzling and ominous light, but no words crossed their trembling lips. Oh, the horror of their position! And already other voices were mingled with those of the assailants; and every one was shouting from without, praying them to open the door, and be saved from their tremendous peril.

'I'll not open the door!' said Mr. Wyley from within; 'they will rob and murder me. They are come to kill me, and I may as well die here. There's no help.'

'There is help, dear uncle!' cried Miss Anne; 'there are other people from Botfield; and help is coming from Longville. Oh, let me in!'

'No,' said the master, 'they all hate me. They'll kill me, and say it was done in the fire. I'll not open to anybody.'

She prayed and expostulated in vain; he cared little for their danger, so hardened was he by a selfish fear for himself. The fire was gaining ground quickly, for a brisk wind had sprung up, and the long-seasoned timber in the old walls burnt like touchwood. The servant lay insensible on the threshold of the master's chamber; and Miss Anne and Stephen looked out from a front casement upon the gathering crowd, who implored them, with frenzied earnestness, to throw open the door.

'Miss Anne,' cried Stephen, 'you can get through the pantry window; you are little enough. Oh, be quick, and let me see you safe!'

'I cannot,' she answered: 'not yet! Not till the last moment. I dare not leave my uncle and that poor girl. Oh, Stephen, if Martha would but come!'

She rested her head against the casement, sobbing, as though her grief could not be assuaged. Stephen felt heart-sick with his intense longing for the arrival of help from Longville, as he watched the progress of the fire; but at last, after what appeared ages of waiting, they heard a shout in the distance, and saw a little band of horsemen galloping up to the burning house.

'They are come from Longville, uncle,' cried Miss Anne. 'You must open now; there is not a moment to spare. The fire is gaining upon us fast.'

He had seen their approach himself, and now he opened the doors, and gave the keys to Miss Anne. He had collected all his papers and notes in one large bundle, which he had clasped in his arms; and as soon as the crowd swept in through the open doors, he cried aloud to the constable from Longville to come and guard him. There was very little time for saving anything out of the house, for before long the flames gathered such volume and strength as to drive every one out before them; and as Stephen stood beside the miserable old man, who was shivering in the bitter night wind, he beheld his dwelling destroyed as suddenly and entirely as the hut at Fern's Hollow had been.


CHAPTER XX

STEPHEN'S TESTIMONY

Mr. Wyley would not stir from the place where he could gaze upon his old home burning to the ground. He stood rooted to the spot, like one fascinated and enchained by a power he could not resist, grasping his precious bundle to his breast, and clinging firmly to the arm of the Longville doctor, who had been one of those who hastened to his rescue. Now and then he broke out into a deep cry, which he did not seem to hear himself; but even the grey dawn of the morning, brightening over the rounded outlines of the mountains, did not awaken him from his trance of terror and bewilderment. Miss Anne kept near to him all night, and Stephen lingered about her, making a seat for her upon the grass, and taking care that Martha also should be at hand to wait upon her. There was a great buzzing of people about them, hurrying to and fro; and every now and then they heard different conjectures as to how the fire began. But it was not, generally known that the constables from Longville and Botfield had contrived to arrest Black Thompson and Davies in the midst of the confusion, and had quietly taken them off to the jail at Longville. When the daylight grew strong, it shone upon a smouldering mass of ruins, and heaps of broken furniture piled upon the down-trodden grass. The master had grown aged in that one night, and he gazed helplessly about him, as if for some one to direct and guide him. He no longer refused to quit the place, only he would not trust himself anywhere near Botfield; and as soon as a carriage could be procured, he and Miss Anne were driven off to Longville. There was nothing more to wait for now; and Stephen went quietly home to breakfast in the cinder-hill cabin.

It was a good deal later than usual that morning when the engineman at the works sent down the first skip-load of colliers into the pit. Four of their number were absent, but that excited no surprise after the events of the night; and even Bess Thompson supposed her father had gone off to the public-house with the others. But what was the amazement of the colliers when they found Tim at the bottom of the shaft, fiercely hungry after his night's fasting, and as fiercely anxious to hear what had been taking place overhead. He had the prudence, however, to listen to their revelations without making any of his own, and would not even explain how he came to be left behind in the pit. He went up in the ascending skip, and, escaping from the curiosity of the people on the bank, he darted as straight as an arrow to Stephen's cabin.

'I'm nigh clemmed,' were his first words, as he seized the brown loaf and cut off a slice, which he devoured ravenously. 'It seems like a year,' he continued; 'thee'lt never catch me being left behind anywhere again. Eh, Stephen, lad! many a time I shouted for fear I'd never see daylight again; it's awful down there in the night. Thee hears them as thee can't see punning agen the coal; and then there comes a downfall like a clap of thunder. I wasn't so much afeared of little Nan: she never did any harm when she was alive; and I thought God was too good to send her out of heaven just to terrify a poor lad like me.'

'But how did thee get left behind?' asked Martha.

Then Tim told them how the horse-doctor had gone down to secure one of the ponies in a large, strong net, in order to bring it to the surface of the earth for a time; and that he had gone down with him more for his own amusement than to help him. He had wandered a little way into the winding galleries of the pit, and came back just as the skip was going up for the last time but one. Thompson and Davies were deep in conversation with the men who remained, and, stealing behind them, he overheard their plot, and their intention of persuading Stephen to join them. After that he dare not for his very life come forward when the skip descended, and he watched them go up, leaving him alone for the night in that dismal place. He had his father's lamp with him, and so made his way to the bottom of the old shaft, and waited, with what impatience and anxiety we may imagine, to hear Stephen return from his work.

'It was awfully lonesome,' he said, 'and I thought Stephen would never come, or I'd never make him hear. It wasn't much better after he had come, only for thinking Miss Anne would be safe. My lamp went out, and I reckon I said "Our Father" over a hundred times. Besides, I was wondering what was being done overhead. I'll never be left behind anywhere again, I can tell ye.'

'Well,' said Stephen, 'my sheep and lambs don't know about the fire, and I must be off. They'll want me just as bad as if I'd been in bed all night.'

Still he could not help turning aside with Tim just for another glimpse of the smouldering ruins, looking so black and desolate in the daylight. But after that he did not loiter a minute, and spent the rest of the morning in diligent attention to his duties, until, a little before mid-day, he saw the farmer who employed him riding across the sheep-walk; and when he ran forward to receive his orders, he bade him make haste and go home to prepare himself for appearing before the magistrate, to give his evidence against Black Thompson and his comrades.

When Stephen reached the cinder-hill cabin he found Tim there again, and Bess Thompson waiting to see him. Poor Bess had been crying bitterly, for by this time it was known that her father and Davies were in jail; though the others, being young and single men, had fled at once from the place, and escaped for the present. As soon as Stephen entered, Bess threw herself on her knees at his feet, and looked up imploringly into his face.

'Oh, dear, good Stephen,' she cried, 'thee canst save father! I'll kneel here till thee has promised to save him. Oh, don't bear any spite agen him, but forgive him and save him!'

'Get up, Bess,' said Stephen kindly; 'don't thee kneel down to a fellow like me. I'll do anything for thy father; I've no spite agen him.'

'Oh, I knew thee would!' she said; 'thee'lt tell the justice thee never saw him there till the other folks came up from Botfield. Tim says he didn't see anybody down in the pit, and he's promised not to swear to their names. Don't thee swear to seeing anybody.'

'But I did see every one of them,' Stephen answered; 'and Tim knew all their voices; and there'll be lots to tell who came up in the last skip.'

'There's nobody in Botfield will swear agen them,' pleaded Bess. 'Whose place is it to know who came up in the last skip, or who was at the fire last night? Oh, Stephen, the Bible says we're to do good to them that hate us. And if father's hated thee, thee canst save him now.'

'Ay,' said Tim, 'Bess is right; there's not a mother's son in Botfield to swear agen them for the master's sake. If he didn't see them, nor Miss Anne, why need we know? I'll soon baffle the justice, I promise ye. It's a rare chance to forgive Black Thompson, anyhow.'

'Bess and Tim,' answered Stephen, in great distress, 'I can't do it. It isn't that I bear a grudge against thy father—I've almost forgotten that he ever did anything to me. But it's not true; it's sure to come out somehow. Why, I don't even know what I said to Miss Anne last night; but if I hadn't told a word to anybody, I'd be bound to tell the truth now.'

'Only say thee aren't certain,' urged Bess.

'Nay, lass,' said Stephen, 'I am certain. I'd do anything that was right for thy sake, and to save thy father; but I can't do this, and it would be no use if I could. God seeth in secret, and He will reward men openly. He's begun to reward the master already. We can do nothing for thy father, but every one of us tell the truth, and pray to God for him.'

'Father was good to thee when thou wert ill,' said Bess.

'Ay, I know it,' he replied; 'but if he was my own father, I could not tell a lie to get him off. I'd do anything I could. Oh, Bess and Tim, don't ask me to go agen the right!'

'It'll break mother's heart,' said Bess, bursting out into a loud crying. 'We made sure of thee, because thee says so much about having thy enemies; and we were only afeared of Tim. Thee says we are to do to another as we'd have them do to us. If thee was in father's place, thee'd want him to do as I ask thee. Thee doesn't think father wants thee to swear agen him?'

'Nay,' answered Stephen, 'the justice and Miss Anne would have me tell the truth. It seems as if I can't do to everybody as they'd like me; so I'll abide by telling the truth.'

There was no time for further discussion, for the constable from Longville came in to conduct them before the magistrate, to give their separate evidence concerning the events of the past night. Bess went with them, weeping all the way beside them, and grieving Stephen's heart by her tears, though she dared not speak a word in the constable's presence. But he gave his testimony gravely and truthfully, and Tim and Martha followed his example; and, in consequence of their joint evidence, Black Thompson and Davies were fully committed to take their trial at the next assizes, and were removed that afternoon to the county jail.

## CHAPTER XXI

### FORGIVENESS

Bess Thompson started off on her way to her desolate home, almost heart-broken, and with such a wrathful resentment against Stephen, and Martha, and Tim, as seemed to blot out all memory of the lessons she had been learning from Miss Anne since the little child's death. She could never bear to go near them, or speak to them again, since they had sworn against her father; and had not he been good to them when Stephen was ill, often sparing her to watch with Martha, as well as helping to make up his wages? If this was their religion, she did not care to have it; for nobody else in Botfield would have done the same. And now she might as well give up all thoughts of getting to heaven, where little Nan and her baby sister were; for there would be nobody to care for her, and she would be obliged to go back to all her old ways.

These were her bitter thoughts as she walked homewards alone, for Stephen was gone up to the doctor's house to inquire after the master and Miss Anne, and the others were waiting for him in Longville. She heard their voices after a while coming along the turnpike road, and walking quickly as if to overtake her; so she turned aside into a field, and hid herself under a hedge that they might pass by. She crouched down low upon the grass, and covered her red and smarting eyes from the sunshine with her shawl, and then she listened for their footsteps to die away in the distance. But she felt an arm stealing round her, and Martha's voice whispered close in her ear,—

'Bess, dear Bess, thee must not hide thyself from us. We love thee, Bess; and we are sore sorry for thee. Stephen is ever so down-hearted about thee and thy father. Oh, Bess, thee must have no spite at us.'

'Bess,' said Stephen, 'thy father owned I was telling the truth, and said he forgave me for speaking agen him; and he shook hands with me afore he went; and he said, "Stephen, thee be a friend to my poor lass!" and I gave him a sure promise that I would.'

'Nobody'll ever look at me now,' cried Bess; 'nobody'll be friends with me if father's transported.'

'We're thy friends,' answered Stephen, 'and thee has a Father in heaven that cares for thee. Listen, Bess; it will do thee good, and poor old grandfather no harm now. He was transported beyond the seas once; and no one casts it up to him now, nor to us; and haven't we got friends? Cheer up, Bess. Miss Anne says, maybe this very trouble will bring thy father to repentance. He said he'd repent some time; and maybe this will be the very time for him. And Miss Anne sends her kind love to thee and thy mother, and she'll come and see thy mother as soon as she can leave the master.'

Thus comforted, poor sorrowful Bess rose from the ground, and walked on with them to Botfield. Most of the house doors were open, and the women were standing at them in order to waylay them with inquisitive questions; but Stephen's grave and steady face, and the presence of Bess, who walked close beside him, as if there was shelter and protection there, kept them silent; and they were compelled to satisfy their curiosity with secondhand reports. Martha went on with Bess to her own cottage to stay all night with her, and help her to console her broken-hearted mother.

Though Martha was truly sorry for Black Thompson's family, she felt her importance as one of the chief witnesses against him; especially as the cinder-hill cabin was visited, not only by the gossips of Botfield, but by more distinguished persons from all the farmhouses around; and her thrilling narrative of her hazardous journey through Botfield along the high road was listened to with greedy interest. In this foolish talking she lost that true sympathy which she ought to have felt for poor Bess, and forfeited the blessing which would have been given to her own soul. But it was very different with Stephen in his lonely work upon the mountains. There he thought over the crimes and punishment of Black Thompson, until his heart was filled with an unutterable pity and fellow-feeling both towards him and his family; and every night, as he went home from his labour, he turned aside to the cottage, to read to Bess and her mother some portion of the Scriptures which he had chosen for their comfort, out of a pocket Bible given to him by Miss Anne.

About a fortnight after these events Stephen received a visitor upon the uplands, where he was seeking a lamb that had strayed into a dwarf forest of gorse-bushes, and was bleating piteously in its bewilderment. A pleasant-sounding voice called 'Stephen Fern!' and when he got free from the entangling thorns, with the rescued lamb in his arms, who should be waiting for him but the lord of the manor himself! Stephen knew his face again in an instant, and dropped the lamb that he might take off his old cap, while the gentleman smiled at him with a hearty smile.

'I am Danesford, of Danesford,' he said gaily; 'and I believe you are Stephen Fern, of Fern's Hollow. I've brought you a message, my boy. Can you guess what young lady has sent me over the hills after you?'

'Miss Anne,' answered Stephen promptly.

'No; there are other young ladies in the world beside Miss Anne!' replied Mr. Danesford. 'Have you forgotten Miss Lockwood? She has not forgotten you; and we are come home ready to give battle to your enemies, and reinstate you in all your rights. She gives Mr. Lockwood and me no rest until we have got Fern's Hollow, and everything else, for you again.'

'Sir,' said Stephen, and his eyes filled with tears, 'nobody can give me back little Nan.'

'No,' answered Mr. Danesford gravely; 'I know how hardly you have been dealt with, my boy. Tell me truly, is your religion strong enough to enable you to forgive Mr. Wyley indeed? Is it possible that you can forgive him from your heart?'

Stephen was silent, looking down at the heath upon which his feet were pressed, but seeing none of its purple blossoms. It was a question that must not be answered rashly, for even that morning he had glanced down the fatal shaft with a deep yearning after little Nan; and as he passed the ruins of his master's house, his memory had recalled the destruction of the old hut with something of a feeling of triumph.

'Sir,' he said, looking up to him, 'I'm afraid I can't explain myself. You know it was for my sake that the Lord Jesus was killed, yet His Father has forgiven me all my sins; and when I think of that, I can forgive the master even for little Nan's death with all my heart. But I don't always remember it; and then I feel a little glad at the fire. I haven't got much religion yet. I don't know everything that's in the Bible.'

'Yet I could learn some lessons from you, Stephen,' said Mr. Danesford, after a pause. 'What do you suppose I should do if anybody tried to take Danesford Hall from me?'

'I don't know, sir,' answered Stephen.

'Nor do I,' he said, smiling; 'at any rate, they should not have it with my consent. Nor shall anybody take Fern's Hollow from you. I have been down to Longville about it, but Mr. Wyley is too ill to see me. By the way, I told Miss Anne I was coming up the hills after you. She wants to see you, Stephen, as soon as possible after your work is done.'

Mr. Danesford rode on over the hills, and Stephen walked some way beside him, to put him into the nearest path for Danesford. After he was gone he watched earnestly for the evening shadows, and when they stretched far away across the plains, he hastened down to the cabin, and then on to Longville, to his appointed interview with Miss Anne.


CHAPTER XXII

THE MASTER'S DEATHBED

When the master at last consented to leave the sight of his old dwelling burning into blackened heaps, he seemed to care nothing where he might be taken. He was without a home, and almost without a friend. It was not accident merely, but the long-provoked hatred of his people, that had driven him from the old chambers and the old roof which had sheltered him for so many years, and where all the habits and memories of his life centred. Miss Anne had not been long enough at Botfield to form friendships on her own account, except among the poor and ignorant people on her uncle's works; and she accepted most thankfully the offer of the doctor from Longville to give them a refuge in his house. No sooner had they arrived there than it was discovered that the master was struck with paralysis, brought on by the shock of the fire, and all the terrifying circumstances attending it. He was carried at once to a bedroom, and from that time Miss Anne had been fully occupied in nursing him.

He had seemed to be getting better the last day or two, and his power of speech had returned, though he spoke but rarely; only following Miss Anne's movements with earnest eyes, and hardly suffering her to leave him; even for necessary rest and refreshment. All that afternoon he had been tossing his restless head from side to side, uttering deep, low groans, and murmuring now and then to himself words which Miss Anne could not understand. She looked white and ill herself, as if her strength were nearly exhausted; but after the doctor had been in, and, feeling the master's pulse, shook his head solemnly, she would not consent to leave his bedside for any length of time.

'How long?' she whispered, going with the doctor to the outside of the door.

'Not more than twenty-four hours,' was the answer.

'Will he be conscious all the time?' she asked again.

'I cannot tell certainly,' replied the doctor, 'but most probably not.'

Only twenty-four hours! One day of swiftly-passing time, and then the eternal future! One more sun-setting, and one more sun-rising, and then everlasting night, or eternal day! For a minute Miss Anne leaned against the doorway, with a fainting spirit. There was so much to do, and so short a space for doing anything. All the real business of the whole life had to be crowded into these few hours, if possible. As she entered the room, her uncle's eyes met hers with a glance of unspeakable anguish, and he called her in a trembling tone to her side.

'I heard,' he whispered. 'Anne, what must be done now?'

'Oh, uncle,' she said, 'have I not told you often, that "Christ Jesus came into the world to save sinners"? There is no limit with God; with him one day is as a thousand years, and He gives you still a day to make your peace with Him.'

'There is no peace for my soul with God,' he answered; 'I've been at enmity with Him all my life; and will He receive me at the last moment? He is too just, too righteous, Anne. I'll not insult Him by offering Him my soul now. You asked me once, "What shall it profit a man if he shall gain the whole world, and lose his own soul?" Mine is lost—lost, and that without remedy. This gold is a millstone about my neck.'

'Uncle,' she said, commanding her voice with a great effort, 'the thief upon the cross beside our Lord had a shorter time than you, for he was to die at sunset that day; yet he repented and believed in the crucified Saviour, who was able to pardon him. Christ is still waiting to forgive; He is stretching out His arms to receive you. Only look at Him with the same penitence and faith that the dying thief felt.'

'Nay,' groaned the dying man, 'he could show his faith by confessing Him before all those who were crucifying the Lord, and it was a glory to the Saviour to forgive him then. But what glory would it be to pardon me on this death-bed, where I can do nothing for Him? No; I can do nothing—nothing! All these years I could have worked for God; but now I can do nothing!'

'Uncle,' said Miss Anne, 'our Lord was asked by some, "What shall we do, that we might work the works of God?" and He answered them, "This is the work of God, that ye believe on Him whom He hath sent." Oh, that is all! Believe on Him, and He will forgive you; and all the angels in heaven will glorify Him for His mercy.'

'Anne,' he answered, fixing on her a look of despair, 'I cannot. My heart is hard and heavy; I remember when it used to feel and care about these things; but it is dead now, and my soul is lost for ever. Anne, even if Jesus is willing to pardon me, I cannot believe in forgiveness.'

Miss Anne sank down by the bedside, unable to answer him, save by a prayer, half aloud, to God for His mercy to be shown to him, if it were possible! He lay there, helpless and hopeless, tossing to and fro upon the pillows. At last he spoke again, in a sharp, clear, energetic tone.

'Anne, be quick!' he said; 'find me my will among those papers. Perhaps if I could do something, I might be able to believe.'

He watched her with impatient eagerness as she turned over the precious parcel of papers which he had rescued from the fire. There were many documents and writings belonging to the property he had gathered together, and it was some time before she could find the will. The master tried to take it from her, but in vain; his right hand was powerless.

'Oh, I forgot!' he cried despairingly; 'this hand is useless, and I cannot alter it now. God will not let me undo the mischief I have done. Anne, I have left Fern's Hollow away from you to my brother Thomas, lest you should restore it to Stephen; and now I can do nothing! Oh, misery, misery! The robbery and murder of the fatherless children rest upon my soul. Send quickly, Anne, send for Stephen Fern.'

Miss Anne sent a messenger to hasten Stephen; and after that the master lay perfectly still, with closed eyes, as if he were treasuring up the little strength remaining to him. The last sunset was over, and the night-lamp was lighted once more; while Miss Anne sat beside him watching, in an agony of prayer to God. There was no sound to be heard, for every one in the house knew that the old man was dying, and they kept a profound quietness throughout all the rooms. He had taken no notice of anything since he asked for Stephen; but when a light rap was heard at the door he opened his eyes, and turned his grey head round anxiously to see whether he was come.

It was Stephen. He stood within the doorway, not liking to enter farther, but looking straight forward at the master with a very pale and sorrowful face, upon which there was no trace of triumph or hatred. Miss Anne gazed earnestly at him, but she did not speak; she would not place herself between him and his dying enemy now.

'Come here, Stephen,' said the master, in a voice of hopeless agony. 'When little Nan was lying dead, you said you would wait, and see what God could do to me. Come near, and hear, and see. Death is nothing, boy; it will be only a glory to you to die. But God is letting loose His terrors upon me; He is mocking at my soul, and laughing at my calamity. Soon, soon I shall be in eternity, without hope, and without God.'

'Oh, master, master,' exclaimed Stephen, 'there is a time yet for our Father to forgive thee! It doesn't take long to forgive! It didn't take even me long to forgive; and oh, how quickly God can do it if you'll only ask Him!'

'Do you forgive me?' asked the master, in astonishment.

'Ah,' he cried, 'I forgave thee long since, directly after I was ill. It was God who helped me; and wouldn't He rather forgive thee Himself? Oh, He loves thee! He taught me how to love thee; and could He do that if He didn't love thee His own self?'

'If I could only believe in being forgiven!' said the dying man.

'Oh, believe it, dear master! See, I am here; I have forgiven thee, and I do love thee. Little Nan can never come back, and yet I love thee, and forgive thee from my very heart. Will not Jesus much more forgive thee?'

'Pray for me, Stephen. Kneel down there, and pray aloud,' he said; and his eyelids closed feebly, and his restless head lay still, as if he had no more power to move it.

'I cannot,' answered Stephen; 'I'm only a poor lad, and I don't know how to do it up loud. Miss Anne will pray for thee.'

'If you have forgiven me, pray to God for me,' murmured the master, opening his eyes again with a look of deep entreaty. Over Stephen's pale face a smile was kindling, a smile of pure, intense love and faith, and the light in his pitying eyes met the master's dying gaze with a gleam of strengthening hope. He clasped the cold hand in both his own, and, kneeling down beside him, he prayed from his very soul, 'Lord, lay not this sin to his charge.'

He could say no more; and Miss Anne, who knelt by him, was silent, except that one sob burst from her lips. The master stirred no more, but lay still, with his numb and paralyzed hand in Stephen's clasp; but in a few minutes he uttered these words, in a tone of mingled entreaty and assertion, 'God be merciful to me a sinner!'

That was all. An hour or two afterwards it was known throughout Longville, and the news was on the way to Botfield, that the master of Botfield works was dead.


CHAPTER XXIII

THE HOME RESTORED

Three months later in the year, when the new house at Fern's Hollow was quite finished, with its dairy and coal-shed, and a stable put up at Mr. Lockwood's desire, a large party assembled within the walls. Martha had been diligently occupied all the week in a grand cleaning down; and Tim and Stephen had been equally busy in clearing away the litter left by the builders, and in restoring the garden to some order. They had been obliged to contrive some temporary seats for their visitors, for the old furniture had not yet been brought up from the cinder-hill cabin; and the only painful thoughts Martha had were the misgiving of its extreme scantiness in their house with six rooms. The pasture before the cottage was now securely enclosed, and the wild ponies neighed over the hedge in vain at the sight of the clear, cool pool where they had been used to quench their thirst; and behind the house there was a plantation of tiny fir-trees bending to and fro in the wind, which they were to resist as they grew larger. Every place was in perfect order; and the front room, which was almost grand enough for a parlour, was beautifully decorated with flowers in honour of the expected guests, who had sent word that they should visit Fern's Hollow that afternoon.

They could be seen far away from the window of the upper storey, which, rising above the brow of the hill behind, commanded a wide view of the mountain plains. They were coming on horseback across the almost pathless uplands; dear Miss Anne, with Mr. Lockwood riding beside her; and a little way behind them the lord of the manor and his young wife, who was no other than Miss Lockwood herself. They greeted Stephen and Martha with many smiles and words of congratulation; and when they were seated in the decorated room, with the door and window opened upon the beautiful landscape, Mr. Lockwood bade them come and sit down with them; while Tim helped the groom to put up the horses in the stable.

'My boy,' said Mr. Lockwood, 'our business is finished at last. Mr. Thomas Wyley will not try his right to Fern's Hollow by law; but we have agreed to give him the £15 paid to your grandfather, and also to pay to him all the actual cost of the work done here. Miss Anne and I have had a quarrel on the subject, but she consents that I shall pay that as a mark of my esteem for you, and my old servant your mother. Mr. Danesford intends to make a gift to you of the pasture and plantation, which were an encroachment upon the manor. And now I want you to take my advice into the bargain. Jackson wants to come here, and offers a rent of £20 a year for the place. Will you let him have it till you are old enough to manage it properly yourself, Stephen?'

'Yes, if you please, sir,' replied Stephen, in some perplexity; for he and Martha had quite concluded that, they should come and live there again themselves.

'Jackson will make a tidy little farm of it for you,' continued Mr. Lockwood. 'My daughter proposes taking Martha into her service, and putting her into the way of learning dairy-work, and many other things of which she is now ignorant. Are you willing, Martha?'

'Oh yes, sir!' said Martha, with a look of admiration at young Mrs. Danesford.

'In this case, Stephen,' Mr. Lockwood went on, 'you will have a yearly income of £20, and we would like to hear what you will do with it?'

'There's grandfather,' said Stephen diffidently.

'Right, my boy!' cried Mr. Lockwood, with a smile of satisfaction; 'well, Miss Anne thinks he would be very comfortable with Mrs. Thompson, and she would be glad of a little money with him. But he cannot live much longer, Stephen; he is very aged, and the doctor thinks he will hardly get over the autumn. So we had better settle what shall be done after grandfather is gone.'

'Sir,' said Stephen, 'I think Martha should have some good of grandmother's work, if she is only a girl. So hadn't the rent better be saved up for her till I'm old enough to come and manage the farm myself?'

Every face in the room glowed with approbation of Stephen's suggestion; and Martha flushed crimson at the very thought of possessing so much money; and visions of future greatness, more than her grandmother had foreseen, passed before her mind.

'Why, Martha will be quite an heiress!' said Mr. Lockwood. 'So she is provided for, and grandfather. And what do you intend to do with yourself, Stephen, till you come back here?'

'I'm strong enough to go back to the pit,' replied Stephen bravely, though inwardly he shrank from it; but how else could the rent of Fern's Hollow be laid by for Martha? 'Now Miss Anne has raised the wages, I should get eight shillings a week, and more as I grow older. I shall do for myself very nicely, thank you, sir; and maybe I could lodge with grandfather at Mrs. Thompson's.'

'No,' said Miss Anne, in her gentle voice, the sweetest voice in the world to Stephen, now little Nan's was silent; 'Stephen is my dear friend, and he must let me act the part of a friend towards him. I wish to send him to live with a good man whom I know, the manager of one of the great works at Netley, where he may learn everything that will be necessary to become my bailiff. I shall want a true, trustworthy agent to look after my interests here, and in a few years Stephen will be old enough to do this for me. He shall attend a good school for a few hours daily, to gain a fitting education; and then what servant could I find more faithful, more true, and more loving than my dear friend Stephen? He can come back here then, if he chooses, and perhaps have Martha for his housekeeper, in their old home at Fern's Hollow.'

'Oh, Miss Anne!' cried Stephen, 'I cannot bear it! May I really be your servant all my life?' and the boy's voice was lost in sobs.

'Come, Stephen,' said the lord of the manor, 'I want you to show us some of your old haunts on the hills. If Miss Anne had not formed a better plan, I should have proposed making you my gamekeeper; for Jones has been telling me about the grouse last year. By the way, if I had thought it would be any pleasure to you, I should have dismissed him from my service for his share in this business; but I knew you would be for begging him in again, so I only told him pretty strongly what a sneak I thought him.'

They went out then across the uplands, a sunny ramble, to all Stephen's favourite places. And it happened that when they reached the solitary yew-tree near which Snip was buried, all the rest strolled on, and left Stephen and Miss Anne alone. Before them, down at the foot of the mountains, there stretched a wide plain many miles across, beautiful with woods and streams; and on the far horizon there hung a light cloud that was always to be seen there, the index of those great works where Stephen was to dwell for some years. Near to them they could discern, in the clear atmosphere, the spires and towers of the county town, where Black Thompson, who had tempted him on these hills, was now imprisoned for many years; and below, though hidden from their sight, was Botfield and the cinder-hill cabin. A band of bilberry-gatherers was coming down the hill with songs and shouts of laughter; and the frightened flocks of sheep stood motionless on the hillocks, ready to flee away in a moment at their approach. Both Miss Anne and Stephen felt a crowd of thoughts, sorrowful and happy, come thronging to their minds.

'Stephen,' said Miss Anne solemnly, 'our Lord says, "When ye shall have done all those things which are commanded you, say, We are unprofitable servants: we have done that which was our duty to do."'

'Yes, Miss Anne,' said Stephen, looking up inquiringly into his teacher's face.

'My dear boy,' she continued, 'are you taking care to say to yourself, "I am an unprofitable servant"?'

'I have not done all those things which are commanded me,' he said simply and earnestly; 'I've done nothing of myself yet. It's you that have taught me, Miss Anne; and God has helped me to learn. I'm afeared partly of going away to Netley; but if you're not there to keep me right, God is everywhere.'

'Stephen,' Miss Anne said, 'you have forgiven all your enemies: Tim, who is now your friend, and the gamekeeper, Black Thompson, and my poor uncle; when you are saying the Lord's Prayer, do you feel as if you should be satisfied for our Father to forgive you your trespasses in the same measure and in the same manner as you have forgiven their trespasses against you?'

'Oh no!' cried Stephen, in a tone of some alarm.

'Tell me why not.'

'It was a rather hard thing for me,' he said; 'it was very hard at first, and I had to be persuaded to it; and every now and then I felt as if I'd take the forgiveness back. I shouldn't like to feel as if our Father found it a hard thing, or repented of it afterwards.'

'No,' answered Miss Anne. 'He is a God "ready to pardon;" and when He has bestowed forgiveness, His "gifts and calling are without repentance." But there is something more, Stephen. Do you not seem in your own mind to know them, and remember them most, by their unkindness and sins towards you? When you think of Black Thompson, is it not more as one who has been your enemy than one whom you love without any remembrance of his faults? And you recollect my uncle as him who drove you away from your own home, and was the cause of little Nan's death. Their offences are forgiven fully, but not forgotten.'

'Can I forget?' murmured Stephen.

'No,' she replied; 'but do you not see that we clothe our enemies with their faults against us? Should our Father do so, should we stand before Him bearing in His sight all our sins, would that forgiveness content us, Stephen?'

'Oh no!' he cried again. 'Tell me, Miss Anne, what will He do for me besides forgiving me?'

'Look, Stephen,' she replied, pointing to the distant sky where the sun was going down amid purple clouds, and bidding him turn to the grey horizon where the sun had risen in the morning; 'listen: "As far as the east is from the west, so far hath He removed our transgressions from us." And again: "He will turn again, He will have compassion upon us; He will subdue our iniquities; and Thou wilt cast all their sins into the depths of the sea." And again: "For I will be merciful to their unrighteousness, and their sins and their iniquities will I remember no more." This is the forgiveness of our Father, Stephen.'

'Oh, how different to mine!' cried Stephen, hiding his face in his hands.

'Yet,' said Miss Anne, 'you may claim the promise made to us by our Lord: "If ye forgive men their trespasses, your heavenly Father will also forgive you," in a far richer measure, with infinite long-suffering, and a multitude of tender mercies.'

'Lord, forgive me, for Jesus Christ's sake!' murmured Stephen.

But the dusk was gathering, and the others were returning to them under the old yew-tree, for there was the long ride over the hills to Danesford, and the time for parting was come. The day was done; and on the morrow new work must be entered upon. The path of the commandments had yet to be trodden, step by step, through temptation and conflict, and weakness and weariness, until the end was reached.

Stephen felt something of this as he walked home for the last time to the cinder-hill cabin; and, taking down the old Bible covered with green baize, read aloud to his grandfather and Martha the chapter his father had taught him on his death-bed; bending his head in deep and humble prayer after he had read the last verse: 'Be ye therefore perfect, even as your Father in heaven is perfect.'


SARAH SMITH (writing as Hesba Stretton) – A CONCISE BIBLIOGRAPHY

Short Stories & Periodicals

The Lucky Leg (19th March 1859)
The Ghost in the Clock Room (Christmas, 1859)
The Postmaster's Daughter (All the Year Round, 5th November 1859)
A Provincial Post Office (All the Year Round, 28 February 1863)
Jessica's First Prayer (Sunday at Home, July 1866)
The Travelling Post-Office (All the Year Round, Mugby Junction, December 1866)
Jessica's Mother (1867)


Books
Fern's Hollow (1864)
Enoch Roden's Training (1865)
The Children of Cloverley (1865)
Jessica's First Prayer (Sunday at Home, July 1866)
The Fishers of Derby Haven (1866)
Jessica's Mother (Periodical 1867, book 1904)
Pilgrim Street (1867)
Little Meg's Children (1868)
Alone in London (1869)
Nellie's Dark Days (1870)
The Doctor's Dilemma (1872)
The King's Servants (1873)
Lost Gip (1873
Cassy (1874)
Brought Home (1875)
In Prison and Out (1878)
Two Secrets (1882)
The Lord's Purse-Bearers (1883)
Sam Franklin's Savings Bank (1888)
Little Meg's Children (1905)
The Christmas Child (1909 in US)


Other Works
Brought Home
Cobwebs And Cables